# Dead Heat

What finally tilted it for Marvin Pike were the accounts discrepancies. Until then he had been prepared to accept the adultery of his partner with his wife, but the discovery that he was being cheated both in business and in bed proved sufficient to tip the scale.

All the same, he wasn't contemplating murder and when Arlene's body went limp in his hands in the course of a particularly bitter row, his first reaction was shock. His second: how to cover his tracks. And how better than by involving his partner, Gareth Somers, by burying Arlene in the grounds of his house?

But when the police called next morning it was not in connection with Arlene's disappearance, which Marvin had prudently reported, but to tell him Somers was dead. Stabbed to death on the patio at about the same time that Marvin had been digging Arlene's shallow grave.

Thereafter nightmare begins for Marvin. Suspected of the murder he has not committed rather than the one he has, his only ally is Gail, his assistant in the shop, who will do anything for him, even lie if need be . . .

Martin Russell's story is full of twists and turns as Marvin wriggles like an eel to escape detection.

# MARTIN *James* RUSSELL

# Dead Heat

M

THE CRIME CLUB

COLLINS, 8 GRAFTON STREET, LONDON W1

William Collins Sons & Co. Ltd
London · Glasgow · Sydney · Auckland
Toronto · Johannesburg

First published 1986
© Martin Russell 1986

British Library Cataloguing in Publication Data

Russell, Martin
    Dead heat.—(Crime Club)
    I. Title
    823'.914[F]     PR6068.U86
    ISBN 0 00 232075 4

Photoset in Linotron Baskerville by
Rowland Phototypesetting Ltd
Bury St Edmunds, Suffolk
Printed in Great Britain by
William Collins Sons & Co. Ltd, Glasgow

# CHAPTER 1

What finally tilted it for Marvin Pike were the accounts discrepancies.

Until then he had been prepared—not eager but willing —to accept if not condone the adultery of his business partner with his wife, exonerating himself from self-accusations of spinelessness with the thought that the material welfare of the three of them took precedence over his personal, self-centred emotional fulfilment. The discovery that on neither level had his associate been playing square with him proved sufficient to tip the scale.

Cuckoldry was one thing. Thinly-concealed contempt for his grasp of financial matters was altogether something else. Pike took a realistic view of his own capabilities, but he had never cared for being derisively underrated by others.

Not, he had to admit, that his uncovering of the deficit owed much to any particular acuteness of perception on his part. It was Gail, his counter assistant, who first pointed him in the right direction with a semi-idle remark about stock shortages. What were her actual words?

'Not doing so good for stationery, we're not. Thought we had plenty, but it's nearly all gone. Shall I get Gareth to order some more?'

Inside Pike's skull, alarm bells had crashed into a bob major peal that had sent him dizzy. Stationery? Enough had been laid in, at summer prices, to see them half way through autumn. Sales, according to the accounts, had been sluggish. Why, then, had stocks so drastically diminished? What had become of the stuff?

Pike set aside an evening—one of those evenings during which Arlene was out at her mysterious 'night class' which had a habit of living up to its name by continuing until the improbable hour of eleven-thirty or beyond—to carry out a thorough examination of the figures and compare them with the few remaining boxes of ballpens, jotting pads and sticky labels that lay about the stockroom at the rear of the shop. The conclusion he reached was stark, inescapable. Profits from the sale of that which had vanished had failed to show up where they should have done. And the sole person in a position to perpetrate and disguise such a procedure was his partner, Gareth Somers.

The culpability of the man was unquestionable. He it was who did the ordering, saw in the deliveries. Pike had always been content to leave that part of the business to him, trusting their mutual interest in the shop's prosperity to maximize his partner's devotion to efficiency in the matter. Only now did he perceive that Somers had in truth carried out his task with a fervour well in excess of requirements. How much stock, Pike asked himself giddily, had been diverted gainfully to other sources? How long had it been going on?

Hunched over his all-purpose table in the living-room, Pike felt the trembling commence in his hands and spread to every part of his anatomy.

The extent and duration of the swindle hardly mattered now. The damage had been done. Already, Pike had been deprived of his wife: now he was being robbed of his livelihood. Only one course was open to him.

When he could focus again, he glanced at the wall-clock. He had two hours, minimum, before Arlene's return from 'night class' was to be expected. Time which could be put to good use.

Scraping his chair round to face his favourite vintage car print hanging over the dresser, he bunched both sets of knuckles under his chin and immersed himself in thought.

While Arlene was undressing for bed, Pike, who was already on his back between the sheets, put a question to her.

'Pick up any new skills, this time?'

'What did you say?'

'Skills. Learn anything fresh?'

A snort came from her direction. Disdain, or an attempt to suppress mirth? In the half-darkness, Pike couldn't decide. It might even have been a noise wrenched from her by the struggle to free herself from the embrace of the close-fitting silk sweater in which she had chosen to attend an instruction period in motor mechanics. Finally hauling it clear of her coppery hair, she draped the garment over the back of a chair and turned her attention to her skirt zip. None of her actions was visible to Pike, but he knew the sound of them by heart. Arlene was a creature of routine.

'I know something,' she said, 'about fuel-injection, if that's anything.'

Ignoring the shameless *double-entendre*, Pike kept his voice mild. 'How long does this course go on?'

'Quite some while.' The skirt followed the sweater.

'Taking anything else, after?'

'Might. Haven't decided.'

'Book-keeping. You could try that.'

'Why?'

'Why not? Be a handy qualification.'

'Meaning I could help out with the accounts? Thanks, but I've enough to do in the house, as it is.' Shadowy wriggling movements suggested that Arlene was divesting herself of her pants. 'Anyway, Gareth sees to all that, I thought you said.'

'He certainly does.' Pike waited a moment. 'Still, he might

appreciate a break from it, now and then. Must get a bit taxing sometimes, shuffling the figures.'

Arlene made no comment. Motionless on his back, forearms pillowing his neck, Pike did his frustrating best to track her movements in the gloom. Although the room was never quite dark, because of the intrusion from a street lamp outside, it was never, at bedtime, fully illuminated either, since Arlene regarded the removal of attire as a task best accomplished out of the spotlight. In home conditions, at least. What she got up to elsewhere was another matter.

'If you're keeping on with the car maintenance,' he resumed presently, 'you might try servicing the van, once in a while. Save us these dirty great bills from the garage.'

'When I'm up to it.'

'You've been at it nearly a year. If you're not qualified yet—'

'Aren't you going to sleep?' she inquired, stepping daintily into pyjama-bottoms while half-concealed behind the open door of the wardrobe. The house, an early-Edwardian terraced fragment, lacked such refinements as built-in closets, and Pike had never got around to having them added. In other circumstances, he wouldn't have hesitated. As things stood, he could be doing it for someone else's benefit. Pike saw no sense in that.

'Not sleepy,' he informed her.

'Obviously not working hard enough. Speaking for myself, I'm nearly out on my feet.' Sliding her arms into the sleeves of her pyjama-top, Arlene emerged from the shelter of the door and completed the buttoning-up process as she padded across to her bed, the twin of his, in the diametrically opposite corner of the room. In a two-bedroomed house they would, Pike knew, have been sleeping with walls between them by now. 'So I'll say good night, and try not to make a racket when you get up in the morning. Five o'clock may be your time, but it's not everybody's.'

'Early to bed, early to rise . . .'

'Makes you a plutocrat—I don't think.' The mattress expostulated tinnily as she worked herself into a recumbent position with a series of muted puffs and sighs.

'Wait for it,' he advised.

'A girl can get tired of waiting.'

'A girl, maybe. You're a mature woman, Arlene. People of our experience don't expect fortunes overnight.'

'Just as well, if you ask me. Now shut up and let me doze off.'

'Before you do . . . can you help out in the shop tomorrow?'

'No, I can't.'

'Why not?'

'Because I've things to see to, back here. And I'm having my hair done in the afternoon.'

'Oh, well. Can't upset those arrangements, can we? Let us know, won't you, when you can spare the odd five minutes.'

'Go to sleep. I'm not answering any more questions.'

'You never answer any, my girl.' Pike didn't say it audibly. He mumbled the words into the pillow as he turned on to his side in what he knew would be a futile quest for oblivion, doomed to be foiled by marauding forces in the shape of multiple distractions—the trading outlook, fiscal problems, his partnership with Somers. They swarmed down every night to lay siege. By now, he supposed, he should have been getting used to them, ready with counterstrokes. Nothing seemed to work.

Three years ago, when he and Somers had agreed on the joint venture, the single-fronted retail premises on the main shopping parade within a mile of Chipperford town centre had seemed to Pike to represent a launch-pad, an escape in one crackling ball of fire from the gravitational chains of industrial recession, employer indifference, lack of opportunity. Nothing, he had thought, could hold them back. And for nine months, a year, they had indeed appeared to be on course for a stable orbit, boosted by the dual rocket-motors of business loans and hard work. After an initial lull of appraisal, people in the locality had begun to show signs of accepting them, dropping in to buy their morning papers, their occasional writing pads and paperback novels, their packets of twenty, in sufficient numbers to justify cautious optimism that one stage of the launch vehicle might soon be jettisoned and the other throttled back. A bare twenty-four months previously, things had started to look rosy.

And now?

Somehow it had all turned sour. In commercial terms, Margar Newsagents were not yet in extreme difficulties; but by no stretch of the truth could the firm be said to be on target or anywhere near it. Or so Somers averred, and Somers after all was the figures man. He it was to whom Pike had entrusted the keeping of the books, the steering of the expedition into a viable flight-path. For a while, as they lifted off, the arrangement had seemed to be a sound one. Then came the meteorite storm.

For the past couple of years, Margar had taken a battering. Somers said so, and he was the expert: he should know.

In view of this, what had puzzled Pike all along was the way in which his partner had contrived to maintain a personal lifestyle that could only be described as rounded, verging upon obese, when avowedly he, like Pike, had been taking so little for his own needs out of such profit as accrued from the business. Scraping along, guarding every penny, Pike had observed with mounting bewilderment and more than a touch of resentment the ability of his associate to acquire the latest in videos, the trendiest in footwear, the ultimate in high-performance three-litre saloons, without visible sacrifice of the frills in life, such as eating. Somers, he had concluded, must have a knack of marshalling resources that was denied to lesser mortals.

Admittedly the guy had had the foresight to remain single. That made a difference. Nobody could dispute it. Marriage meant compromise, the trimming of material objectives. Everyone said so.

For all that . . .

The doubts had remained, until this evening. This evening, Pike's eyes had finally been opened. And that, he reflected bitterly, in a literal sense was the way they were destined to remain for the rest of this particular night: fixed, staring, untouched by the feelers of slumber. Pike, by now, knew all about insomnia. He could have written a manual on the subject. Maybe he would, once this phase of his existence was safely behind him.

From the other bed came a sigh. Arlene turned over.

What was she dreaming?

Partly against his will, Pike tried to guess. Into every fevered image that his brain conjured up, the fleshy visage of Somers somehow managed to loom; Pike couldn't get rid of it. He had, as it happened, always rather envied his partner's looks. In a weird way, he had appreciated from the outset just what Arlene saw in the bloke. It would not have been overstretching the matter to say that, even now, he almost sympathized with her.

When all was said and done, the choice she had made nine years ago could hardly, from her point of view, be described as a winner. Pike, who tried to be fair-minded when he had the energy, was obliged to concede the point.

What was it, precisely, he had said to her at the time that had thrown the vital switch?

He had total recall of the dialogue. His share of it had been assiduously rehearsed, fluently delivered, a theatrical performance worthy of his talents. The notion of a stage career had appealed to Pike during his formative years. An otherwise colourless academic progress had been highlighted, for him, by appearances in productions of the school

dramatic society: walk-on parts, mostly, but deeply fulfilling
to a would-be Thespian who shrank from exposing his real
ambition to a derisive circle of family and friends. He knew
he could act. Ever since childhood, he had in effect been
playing a role; perhaps a variety of roles. Beneath it all
lurked the real Pike, and yet he could never put a finger on
the character. A substitute was always in command. As it
had been nine years ago, with Arlene.

'By the time I'm thirty,' Pike had remarked, as they
sauntered on the towpath of the sepia stream that flowed
oilily through the Chipperford outskirts, 'I'll be out of this
dump. I'll be a millionaire.'

'Oh yeah?' To Pike's finely-tuned ear, the automatic
surface mockery of Arlene's retort seemed to hide traces of
wariness, a reluctance to dismiss such a claim out of hand.
'So what d'you plan on doing? Robbing a bank?'

The rhythmic shake of Pike's head conveyed its own
message of sober, copper-bottomed conviction. 'If you know
what you're up to,' he murmured, gazing out with a certain
jut-jawed mistiness across the water, 'there's no problem
about making a fortune. Anyone can do it. Time-scale might
be a different proposition. Some people . . . it can take 'em
a lifetime to get where they want.'

'You're different, of course.'

'Me? I prefer short cuts.'

'Whenever I try a short cut,' Arlene said crushingly, 'I
get lost.'

'That's because you don't take the precaution of consulting the map.'

'Which map are you talking about?'

Pike smiled. 'Trade secret.'

They walked a little further. An angler on the opposite bank
remained indifferent to their passing. Seeming to observe him
and his equipment, Arlene said casually, 'There can't be many
trades that'll guarantee a million, just like that.'

Pike knew at that moment that he had her. 'Any under-
taking will do. It's what you bring to it, as an individual.
Come back and see me, Arlene, in ten years' time. I'll
scribble you a cheque for any amount you like.'

'Yes, but will I be able to cash it?'

Another smile. 'You can always try.'

A skiff, propelled by two bunched oarsmen lost in their
world of ferocious dedication, streaked past upstream.
Arlene watched them out of sight.

'If you did make a million, what would you do with it?'

'Spend it.'

'On yourself, I suppose.'

'Me and whoever I happened to be with at the time. Cash
is for enjoying, I reckon. Having fun.'

She turned to face him. 'I believe you're serious. You
honestly think you're going to be loaded.'

'Wrong,' he replied simply. 'I *know* I'm going to be.'

'What about setbacks? Ill health. Bad luck. Errors of—'

'I'm in good health and I don't make mistakes. Bad luck
you can overcome. No use, Arlene,' he said on a playful
note. 'You can't argue with a statement of fact. One decade
from now, I'll be paying more each year in tax than your
dad earns in a lifetime.'

'Big-head.'

Despite her concluding insult, Arlene seemed pensive for
the rest of the day. When, at the end of it, Pike suggested a
weekend outing, she assented with noticeably less coaxing
than usual, affording him private amusement as well as
gratification. Girls, he decided, were ridiculously easy meat.
Sheer passive prey, begging to be caught and slaughtered.
On the Saturday, they visited a stately home, had tea in the
grounds, went to a cinema in Oxford, and agreed upon
matrimony as they rode home in the train. Although they
had the compartment to themselves, Arlene showed a disin-
clination to seal the contract with more than a token peck

or two on Pike's left cheek; lacking the self-confidence to assert himself, he left it at that for the moment. Time, he reasoned, was on his side. As he prospered, so Arlene's malleability could be expected to develop. One thing pursued another.

On one score, Pike nursed few illusions. Animal magnetism alone, he was aware, would never achieve for him his heart's desire. Physically, he had been short-changed by nature. The retreating hairline, irregular nose, weak mouth and botched dental structure were all against him. Unfair, but there it was. A fellow had to make the best of such assets as he had. These, in Pike's case, comprised a persuasive loquacity and a strong belief in his own commercial judgement, sufficient in total to paint, for the time being, an impressive gloss upon his remarks. Arlene had been captured: so far, so good. Work, however, remained to be done.

Nine years and much arduous toil later, Pike had begun to face up to the fact that he might have miscalculated.


CHAPTER 2

'So you won't be coming into the shop this morning?'

'Not if you want the housework done. Or a meal when you get home.'

Arlene seldom bothered herself with breakfast. Pike found this irritating. He liked the full routine: cereals, egg, sausage and bacon, soft rolls, toast, honey. Coffee by the half-pint. Breakfast, in his opinion, was a ritual to be savoured, a flying start to the day. To see Arlene sipping from a cupful of lemon tea while clipping her fingernails on the sofa—out of range of what she clearly regarded as his animalistic gorgings at the table—gave him the uncomfortable sensation of being on display, a gross exhibit in a weight-watchers' aversion therapy demonstration.

Stubbornly, he refused to vary his habits. If Arlene wanted to eat like a sparrow, that was her premature funeral. He did wonder, occasionally, how anybody could starve herself most of the time and yet retain a figure like hers: it seemed a biological contradiction. Maybe she put away more than she ever let on. It would be in line with her secretive ways.

'Gareth,' he said slyly, 'will be disappointed.'

'Why Gareth?'

'When he's there—which isn't often—he likes having a bit of female talent around.'

'There's Gail,' Arlene said indifferently, frowning at the outstretched fingers of her left hand before attacking the nails with a file. 'She's feminine enough, I'd have thought.'

'Gareth's used to her.'

'If I made a practice of turning up, he'd be used to me. Novelty. That's all you ever think of, you fellahs.' She applied nail varnish.

'Some of us do have other thoughts.'

Sinking his teeth into the soft centre of a honey-smeared bread roll, Pike commenced abstractedly to chew. Arlene's calm, hazel-eyed gaze was, he knew, full upon him, record-ing every rotation of his jaws. He wished he could have stared her down, but he had tried it before and emerged the loser. Arlene could out-stare most people. Not, he felt certain, because of any inner strength or self-conviction: it was just another of those knacks with which she came ready-equipped. When he sensed that she had returned to the more absorbing study of her finger-ends, he took another bite out of the roll and hauled the *Daily Mail* nearer to his plate.

'Here's something,' he remarked presently.

'Read it out, then. If you have to.'

'*New Deal for Small Businesses. Discretionary loans are to be*

*made available to traders in need of expansion capital. Funded by a*
*central government grant—'*

'I read that,' she interrupted. 'Last night. In the *Echo.'*

'Oh? You had time to look at the evening paper?'

The stare travelled back to his face. 'Someone at the class
had a copy. I grabbed it during coffee-break.'

'Sounds to me more like a rave-up than further education.'
Pike took a gulp of his own coffee. 'Well? What d'you
reckon?'

'What do I reckon about what?'

'The scheme,' he said testily. 'Cash handouts.'

'Wouldn't touch it,' she said decisively. 'They'd only want
the money back, a year later. Plus interest, probably.'

'They're not that stupid. If they did it that way—'

'It's the only way their minds work. Mug's game, if you
want my opinion.'

'What do you know about it?' Pike had little time for
governments of any political complexion, but Arlene's scornful dismissal of the idea somehow incensed him.

'As much as you do, I bet. Who pays the household bills?
Who does the shopping? If I don't know how to juggle the
pennies—'

'It's not pennies we're talking about.'

'No. Exactly. That's what worries me.'

Pike put his cup down with a clatter. 'Meaning?'

'Meaning you're just the type they're aiming at. Dish out
a thousand or two, here and there; put a sparkle on the
economy for a few weeks; then leave you to stew in your
own debts. It's as clear as daylight.'

'What a load of twaddle. Shows how much you know
about me.'

'I know as much as I need to, thanks very much.
Anyway . . .' Arlene paused in her nail-scraping to examine
him more intently. 'What would you want with a loan? Not
thinking of expanding, are you?'

'Why not?'

She directed a pitying smile at the varnish bottle. 'You can't even make a go of what you've got. If you've still got delusions of that million by the time you're—'

'Don't keep on about it.'

'Why shouldn't I? You always did.'

'All right, then,' said Pike, stung. 'I could still do it, if I wasn't being held back.'

'Who's holding you back?' For the first time in weeks, Arlene seemed genuinely to be attending to what he was saying. 'Who is it you're talking about? Me?'

'Not you.'

'Who, then? Somebody I know?'

Cowardice tweaked Pike back from the brink. 'Don't forget,' he temporized, 'we've got competition, nine shops away. This Indian bunch—'

'Pakistanis.'

'Pakis, have it your way. They started up six months ago, right? First thing they did, they slashed prices. Twenty per cent off this, thirty off that—you name it, they're giving it away. Proper Eastern bazaar, it is, along there. Result: they've filched half our trade. When they've put us out of business—'

'Why not cut *your* prices?'

'We can't. We'd be broke in a month. They can obviously stand it, for a while; they've probably got half a dozen other shops behind 'em. So the idea is, they keep on with the price war till we go under, then when they've got the monopoly of the area—'

'If you can't reduce the things you're selling,' said Arlene on a note of fatigue, 'what's to stop you branching out a bit? They're the sub-Post Office, aren't they, as well as a general store? Well then. They can't take on more than a certain amount. There's your chance to stock a few extra lines— the kind they haven't the space for. That way, you could—'

'What have I just been saying?' demanded Pike in triumph. 'Expansion. If I got a loan, I could do it, right? Stands to reason.'

Arlene surveyed him frowningly. 'You mean, *we* could do it.'

'No.' Taking a breath, he returned her gaze with a dash of defiance. 'I'm talking about me.'

'Drop Gareth?'

'By heading off on my own, I'd be in a different position, wouldn't I? For a start, all the profit I made I could keep. None of this fifty-fifty rubbish. That's the real mug's game, if it's *my* opinion you're after.'

Arlene's face had lost most of its colour. Visibly she was struggling for words. 'You seem to need reminding,' she said at last, 'that you've got an agreement. You went into this together—remember? Margar. It's both of you, each making a separate contribution. You chatting up the customers, Gareth looking after the accounts . . .'

'He's not the only accountant in Chipperford. I can employ anybody on a consultative basis. They don't have to be my partner.'

He felt rather pleased with the word 'consultative.' Whether Arlene was impressed or otherwise, he couldn't gauge. For the moment she seemed to be caught flat-footed. Her stunned reaction should have given Pike satisfaction; had it been attributable solely to dismay on their joint behalf over Margar's fragile prospects, he would undoubtedly have felt a warm glow of pleasure at the depth of her response. Unfortunately, as he knew, it went some distance beyond that. In any case, he wasn't fooled. Arlene's resilience had shaken him before.

She rose duly to the challenge. 'I never heard anything so wet,' she announced, screwing the cap viciously back on to the varnish container. 'Without Gareth you'd be nothing. You'd be bankrupt before you could turn round. Besides, there's the legal aspect. You can't just back out of a partnership. If you tried to wriggle clear, Gareth could take you to court. And he would, too. Then you'd finish up without a share in anything at all. Is this what you want?'

Pike eyed her broodingly.

'He couldn't, you know. He'd be in no position to call in the law.'

During the years they had been at school together, Somers had always been the smart one. So marked was the contrast that Pike, when he thought about it, marvelled at the popular conception of them as a twosome: rightfully, he felt, Somers should have had no time for the low-intellect form of companionship which was all that someone of Pike's capacity could provide. Only later, dimly, did the other's motivation dawn upon him. Somers had used him as a beauty uses a drab, to highlight her own qualities.

He could, he supposed, have felt bitter about it. In reality, the chief emotion he had since experienced was that of doglike gratitude for the shafts of radiance reflected his way in the course of an otherwise unremarkable scholastic career. Exploitation for selfish purposes was better than no exploitation at all.

When they both left school, Pike treasured no illusions that their association would continue, and in the immediately subsequent years this expectation was confirmed. Somers joined a local firm of auditors and studied for his exams. Pike drifted into the town's lone supermarket and learned how to bilk the customers without letting them feel pain. There was nothing vindictive about it. By nature, Pike was not dishonest. It was simply that the system had become an accepted, an inevitable part of the commercial fabric, and to defy it would have taken moral resolution of a calibre to which he had never laid claim. Apart from which, he had a goal to pursue. Not to have participated in the general affable fraudulence would have amounted to wilful self-deprivation on a major scale.

By the time his path crossed that of Somers once more, Pike by this and other, more legitimate means had accumulated a sizeable hoard of what it pleased him to call 'floating capital' and was looking around for somewhere to cast anchor. His mother having died from liver cirrhosis when he was twelve, he had no parental responsibilities since his father had remarried and moved to Plymouth to run a guest house. Little love being lost between Pike and his stepmother, communication between himself and the pair of them had all but died out. When he and Somers renewed their acquaintance, Pike was living in a rented room over a butcher's shop, part of a bleak parade serving a housing estate that had recently been grafted on to the town's eastern flank, and was working in the grocer's next door. Although this establishment sold only foodstuffs and alcohol, people kept coming in to ask for newspapers and Sellotape. This it was that had given Pike his inspiration.

'What most customers want,' he explained to Somers over a reunion pint at the Grapes, 'is a bit of everything under one roof, but not necessarily a supermarket—right? Somewhere they can nip into, pick up a packet of envelopes, pay for it and leave by the same door: none of this time-wasting checkout nonsense.'

'You're sure about that?'

'What made you come in, this morning?' Pike asked. 'You thought we sold paperbacks. If we'd had any, you'd have picked one, paid for it and gone out happy . . . and we'd have been left pocketing your cash. Multiply that a few times and you get an idea of how we're losing out.'

'I take the point,' Somers said graciously. 'But I thought the age of the corner store was dead.'

'Don't you believe it. Ask our Asian contingent. They seem to do all right.'

'I was about to say—surely they're collaring that particular market?'

'Only because we're letting 'em. For anyone prepared to graft . . .' Pike spoke with the fluency created by the conviction that for once he was talking a kind of sense and that he had his schoolfriend's undivided attention: an almost unprecedented blend of advantages. 'The main proviso, of course,' he added, 'is situation.'

'Obviously important.'

Thirty yards, Pike enlarged, could make all the difference. As it happened, he'd seen some empty premises that very afternoon and they were ideal. Practically next-door to a takeaway and the right side of the bus stop, slap on the route to the town centre. 'I asked about the rent, too. Quite reasonable.'

'Rates?'

'Can't avoid 'em, can you? Wherever you choose.' Pike hadn't given a thought to rates. To cover the deficiency he began to talk faster. 'Tell you what, Gareth. If I'd a couple of extra thousand and a spot of reliable help, I'd be signing on the dotted line for that place tomorrow, no messing. It's pure gold. You've got the incoming trade from the estate, *plus* the rest of the catchment area—all those residential streets around the station and the park, must be a couple of square miles minimum. *Plus*, they're mostly upper bracket. Cash in their pockets. Can't miss.'

Somers delivered the faintly superior half-smile that he had cultivated at school as a first line of defence. 'In my experience, it's the upper classes who tend to watch the pennies. The blue-collar workers—they're the big spenders.'

'I'd go some way along with that,' Pike agreed deferentially. 'On the other hand, strictly speaking, it's not the big spenders I'd be chasing. I'm talking about everyday, bread-and-butter purchases, remember. A fast turnover of a lot of small essentials. A service where it's needed. I might be wrong, but I've a gut feeling about this. You need to go a lot by instinct in the retail trade.'

'And you trust your instinct?'

'Have to, don't I?' Pike smiled self-deprecatingly. 'It's all I've got.'

'Don't undersell yourself,' Somers said politely. He was looking thoughtful. 'How far,' he asked presently, 'is this place?'

Pike jumped up. 'Want to see it?'

On the way, Somers explained to Pike that he felt he had arrived at a career crossroads. Understretched in his present post, he had no consuming wish to move to lusher pastures such as Birmingham or south to London. 'I like it around here. My friends are in the area and I've got this pad in Beech Chase—coach-house conversion with a nice garden, really secluded. I wouldn't want to decamp. Vocation-wise, though, I do feel in need of a challenge. Auditing other firms' accounts can start getting to you, after a while.'

'I know what you mean.' Pike felt justified in assuming his own inclusion in the circle of friends whom Somers was loath to abandon. 'You feel sometimes you'd like to benefit personally from your efforts. Not pass the gains on to other people.'

'You've hit it, Pikey.' Somers ran the power-assisted steering of his BMW lazily through adroit fingers as he took the corner into Mount Avenue. 'Which place is it?' he asked, scanning the shop frontages on the parade as they cruised past.

Pike pointed. 'The one with the sign up. You can park opposite. Another advantage, see. No yellow line.'

His friend was suitably impressed. An exterior inspection of the premises seemed to do nothing to dissipate his initial favourable reaction, and they arranged to see the agent the following day to obtain the keys. Pike passed the night in a sweat of tension. When, next afternoon, the shop door was opened to them by a representative of Pearce, Unwin and Paterson ('PUP', remarked Somers genially. 'I trust that's not what they're hoping to sell us'), he experienced the same kind of bodily thrill, top to toe, as he had felt on sliding into the driving seat of his first runabout, a corroded Mini with ninety thousand miles on the clock and a tendency to yaw on bends. Except that this one was five times as intense, and accompanied by sensations of faint terror. What was he getting himself into?

Somers, for his part, seemed to have few qualms. Before long, he was prime mover in the negotiations, coaxing the project through. Pike, the instigator, found himself tagging along, agreeing to this and that, scrawling his name on documents, mortgaging his future. When doubts intruded, he squashed them with the reflection that Somers, the figures man, knew just what he was about and could be relied upon to safeguard their interests in the long term, even if the immediate prospect was one of a ferocious workload with a questionable return. Basically, Pike was still in a state of elation. Meeting up again with his school chum had been enough to give him a fillip; finding himself so far accepted as to warrant a joint venture into business was the icing on the cake. If Somers had been less than wholehearted and the idea had fallen through, Pike would still have regarded the episode as one to be treasured in memory.

From first to last, however, Somers betrayed no reservations. A month after their reunion, they sat having more drinks at the Grapes. This time it was a celebration. A lease of the shop premises had just been signed and Margar Newsagents were in business, capitalized to the tune of seven thousand pounds; five thousand of which came from Pike, which was why his portion of the new firm's title had received top billing. It was the first time he could recall ever having led Somers in anything.

Arlene, too, was there. She had known Somers during their schooldays.

'I always thought you were proper stand-offish,' Somers ribbed her, after they had toasted Margar's future prosperity.

'Dare say I was.' She sent him a lateral look that jerked the first minuscule quiver of uneasiness into Pike's chest. 'You and your horrible little mates were always trying to fetch us down a peg.'

'I don't remember that.'

'Boys don't care, do they? Means nothing to them. Just a bit of fun.'

'*Men* care,' Somers said profoundly.

The first months of the enterprise were chequered though exhilarating. Most of their capital went on laying in stock. Here, Pike's retailing experience proved its worth. He knew what was needed, in what quantities, from which sources and how often. When a line they hadn't got was asked for, he got Somers to order it and gave prominence to its display. He made Arlene wear a bright green scarf in bonnet style on her coppery hair when she served at the counter, so that customers came in for the pleasure of looking at her. In conjunction with a tight-fitting overall of the same hue, it gave her an appearance of country-fresh efficiency. Although the image was not fully matched by her manner—at times she could be of a sulky disposition, so that an applicant for five cigars could be made to feel that he was putting in a tiresome request for a dozen oysters—on balance she was a distinct asset to the venture, and on this purely practical level Pike was proud of her.

Their home life was another matter. This, however, he hoped would improve. Once she knuckled down to things, accepted that her carefree days as the youngest of three children, with indulgent parents, were a thing of the past, she would come fully to appreciate the lustre of the new lifestyle he was offering her and view him in a fresh light.

If this were so, he had to concede presently that it was all going to take time. After the first few weeks, any enthusiasm that Arlene had shown for her counter duties waned noticeably. She devised a series of excellent reasons for staying at home with increasing frequency 'to catch up with the chores'. When Pike objected, she had no hesitation in pointing out that men knew nothing about these things, had no conception of what 'running a house' entailed, and unless he wanted rooms knee-deep in filth, uncooked meals and dirty laundry in every corner, he had better not begrudge her the time necessary to avoid such horrors. Her appearances at the shop dwindled to three days a week; three mornings a week; three days a fortnight. When she did turn up she was sulkier than ever, treated customers with indifference, made errors at the till, and left early. More often than not, Pike found himself coping alone, run off his feet, fighting to retain customer goodwill against odds that mounted steadily against him.

Somers was no help. From the outset, it had been agreed —or tacitly understood—that his role in the partnership was to be that of professional adviser, keeper of the books, observer of the monetary situation, negotiator with suppliers. 'I'm no good, Pikey, selling things. That's your department. Leave the figurework to me and we'll get along famously.'

If progress to date, Pike had since had occasion sourly to reflect, epitomized his partner's notion of fame, then all that could be hoped for was a period of nonentity. Somer, it was true, seemed to devote a great deal of time to 'the books'. He pored over them in the stockroom—barely more than a cubicle—at the rear of the shop, habitually emerging at lunch-time with an executive briefcase, an air of importance, and the proclamation that he was taking the files home for 'a thorough look at the various items' without the retailing

distractions around him, and that he would be back in the
morning. Sometimes this did occur. On other, increasingly
frequent occasions he would telephone to say that he was
'taking up a point or two' with the wholesalers and would
be out for the day.

Pike had no means of checking. His partner's bachelor
existence in a semi-rural residential district several miles
from the town centre meant that his movements were next
to impossible for other people to log—least of all Pike
himself, who was tied unremittingly to the shop and invariably snatched a sandwich for lunch while continuing to
serve jellybabies and birthday cards. An only child, Somers
was on reputedly amiable terms with his parents, who ran
a smallholding on the outskirts of Oxford; but, from what
Pike could gather, they saw little of him. He was too much
on the hop, engrossed with his own affairs. Once or twice,
Pike had contacted them by phone to ask whether they knew
of their son's whereabouts, to no avail. Gareth, Mrs Somers
would say apologetically, was a law unto himself.

Pike never doubted it. One mystery of his partner's existence that never ceased to intrigue him was how he found
the material means to pursue such a course. Whether he
was renting, had bought, or was in process of buying the
converted coach-house in Beech Chase, the fact remained
that in some form or another it had to be paid for, as did the
metallic-coated, hide-upholstered, aerodynamic Mercedes
convertible to which he had graduated from the BMW. At
the age of twenty-nine, Somers was Pike's junior by twelve
days, and as a single man had presumably enjoyed a rela-
tively clear financial passage since leaving school; but when
all was said and done, the local firm with which he had been
stuck for most of that time was hardly one of the plusher
outfits and his earnings could not have been astronomical.
The way he was living now, he must have other sources of
income. A legacy, perhaps, from a rich relative. Or help

from his parents. There were a number of possibilities.

In this case, however, why had his partner's capital contribution to Margar been of such modest proportions? At the time, Pike had rather welcomed it as leaving him at least nominally in the driving seat, morally justified in making the decisions. For some reason that he couldn't define, it hadn't worked out quite like that, and by this time Pike had started to feel vaguely uneasy about the extent of Somers's commitment to the project, even before his discovery of the discrepancies.

Now, all had been made clear. There was no legacy. No parental aid. Somers, for an unknown period of time, lately at the expense of his former schoolfriend, had been living on his wits and being none too scrupulous about it. Pike himself had little to crow about in this respect, but he did set himself standards of a kind. Treachery towards an associate was off-limits.

Especially when it hit profits.

# CHAPTER 3

''Morning, Marve.'

Ballooning into the shop, Gail paused to remove the bicycle clips anchoring the lower half of the white cotton boiler suit in which she was loosely encased. The days of the trim, green smock were long gone. Sartorially speaking, as Pike had been known to put it with heavy humour, anything served nowadays. Straightening in triumph to dump the clips in a vacant corner with a clatter, his assistant added, 'Sorry I'm a bit behind. Mum forgot to call us, so I overslept. Well, says she forgot. Doesn't fancy climbing the stairs, if you ask me, not more than she can help.'

Pike grunted. 'That stack there needs price-tagging.'

'So I missed breakfast.' Seizing a biscuit-centred choc-olate bar, Gail tore off the wrapping and bit hungrily into the confection while slapping her ash-blonde strands into new positions at the mirror behind the pen-rack. 'Never even stopped for coffee. I'm going to be parched before we're even open. Feel like elevenses early this morning?'

'Let's get eight-thirty over with, first.' Hefting a card-board carton of jotting pads from floor to counter, Pike arranged it alongside the sticky labels and returned for another. 'Tell your mother, if she can't face the stairs she should buy a whistle. I'm counting on her.'

'You tell her,' suggested Gail, smearing colour upon her wide lips and scowling at the result. 'I've not got the nerve.'

'Bypass her, then. Book a morning call with British Telecom.'

'Leave it out. Cost a fortune. Not late that often, am I?'

'Or buy yourself a motor for that pushbike. Get you along quicker.'

'I will if you pay for it.' Unruffled, Gail swallowed the last of the chocolate biscuit before grabbing the price-tagger and commencing to stab numerals on to the packs of manilla envelopes piled at the far end of the counter. She stood in no awe of Pike. After eighteen months in Margar's employ, she knew precisely where she stood, how far she could go; she also knew that she had become indispensable. Not that she exploited the fact. Pike gave her this. Sunny by nature, she was also fair-minded and liked to 'play square with them as plays square with me'.

Pike, for all his genial strictures, was painfully aware of his reliance upon her. With the gradual but relentless withdrawal of Arlene from the serving scene, he had been at his wits' end to find suitable help until Gail replied perkily to his small-ad in the local free-sheet and subsequently presented herself, untidy yet personable, with a lively atti-tude that he calculated might commend itself to paying customers more than any amount of starched efficiency. As it turned out, Gail proved to be both vivacious and competent. Having mastered the job, which took her three days, she developed into a natural. Prudently allowing her free rein with her attire—to which nobody seemed to take exception, if they noticed it at all—Pike heaped duties upon her and blessed the day on which she had chanced to pick up a copy of the *Chipperford Record* and catch sight of his urgent plea for 'Smart intelligent girl for interesting post in central locale, salary negotiable.' He now lived in mortal dread of her handing in her notice. It would happen, he was convinced, some time. Somebody would spot her, lure her away. His luck couldn't hold indefinitely.

If Pike had a quibble, it concerned Gail's misuse of his forename. It wasn't, he told himself, that he liked to be pompous. By now they would have been on first-name terms anyway: any stiffer relationship within a retailing oblong eight yards by four could scarcely have survived. In view of the ten-year age difference between them, however, he would have preferred the initiative to have come from himself. As it was, 'Mr Pike' had vanished irretrievably on their second day in harness and it had been Marvin, or on matier occasions the hideous 'Marve', ever since. The latter salutation made him wince physically, but there was nothing to be done about it now. For having Gail around, taking care of everything that managed to slip through his own tightly-cast net, it was a small price to pay.

Somers remained elusive. Despite his assurances, when he did put in an appearance, that he had been 'really chewing up the mileage, old lad' in tireless pursuit of wholesale bargains, or conning ledgers for hours at a stretch, Pike could never make out exactly what his nominal partner was meant to be doing. Accountancy being a mystery to him, Pike had little idea of how many hours in a week should be consumed by a task of this nature. If Somers told him, as he frequently did, that without his cerebral efforts Margar would list and founder in three months, it was difficult for Pike to refute the claim without exposing himself to accusations of dabbling a toe in waters where he was not qualified to swim.

Finally, exasperated beyond endurance, he took action. He signed on at a night class for a basic course in book-keeping and economics.

It wasn't easy. Pike hadn't the brain for this sort of thing, besides which it entailed an appalling rush on two evenings a week to finish off at the shop in time to get to the technical institute on the other side of town. Impelled by resentment, he kept at it doggedly.

Arlene raised surprisingly little demur. He almost had the feeling that his bi-weekly absences were not unwelcome. The suspicion made no contribution to his peace of mind: for all this, he hung on grimly to the end of the course and left with a diploma, Grade Three, certifying—with less than total accuracy—that Pike, M. W., had achieved a grasp of his subject commensurate with the requirements of the examining body and accordingly was entitled to enter for the intermediate course if he so wished.

Pike didn't wish. The elementary syllabus alone had drained him; but at least he could now find his way about a statement of accounts without feeling that he was trying to hack a path through Brazilian jungle with the aid of a blunt kitchen knife. When the time came, he speculated, he might find himself in a better position to find out just what, if anything, Somers was up to. There was no immediate hurry.

Meanwhile, Arlene announced her intention of taking up night classes herself.

Having set the precedent, Pike could hardly voice an objec-tion. But after the first six months he had tentatively begun to suggest at intervals that she might by now have got the thirst

for knowledge out of her system. Calmly ignoring him, Arlene
had continued to disappear on two evenings a week, Tuesday
and Thursday, and there was still no sign of the regimen's
coming to an end. Pike's early restiveness had deepened to
frustration. In these days of the liberated female, however,
there seemed little he could do. Arlene's right to extend herself
mentally was as irrefutable as his own, albeit the course she
had chosen was of debatable merit.

'Arlene not coming today?' Gail inquired artlessly, price-
tagging the final envelope and turning her attention to the
adjacent balls of string.

Pike replied with another grunt.

'My dad's always on at me to learn somethink.' Gail
made rueful adjustments to the price-tagger. 'You know,
useful like. Can't think what, though.'

'Karate?' he suggested.

She tittered. 'Might come in handy against the muggers.
Bit rough for me. Arlene does car maintenance, doesn't she?
I could try that.'

'So you are thinking of getting motorized?'

'No, I'm not. Quite happy with the bike. Anyway I
couldn't afford it, not on what you pay us.'

'Nobody,' Pike said dispassionately, 'can *afford* to run a
vehicle. We just do it, and to hell with the consequences.
Mind you, some of us have to draw the line. If I could *afford*
it,' he said half-dreamily, 'I'd swap the van for a new estate
of some kind—a Peugot, maybe. They're nice. But you have
to be realistic.'

Gail nodded approval. 'There's running costs and
everythink, isn't there, on top of what you pay to start with.
Does Arlene do the servicing on your van?'

'She checks the tyre pressures,' Pike said drily, 'and tops
up the oil levels.'

'Oh, well. Once she's finished the course, she'll probably
do the lot. How long she's been at it, now?'

'Bloody ages.'

Gail slid him a look of feminine appraisal. 'Gets her out of the house,' she said diplomatically, 'of an evening. I reckon everyone should have an interest.'

Pike went across to the till. 'Retailing,' he observed, 'isn't necessarily as tedious as all that. If you want to, you can make an interest out of most things.'

Still discreet, Gail kept her silence.

For a while, Pike had genuinely believed that Arlene was attending the technical institute twice weekly to learn how to keep an internal combustion engine in trim. In his naïvety, he had pictured her on arrival, donning overalls, perspiring over spanners. He hadn't even begrudged her the use of the van to get there. Not until that ghastly night in December when he had made his discovery.

Tuesday, December 4, had seen the establishment of a new rainfall record in Chipperford.

In the two hours up to nine-thirty in the evening, more than an inch had descended, and half an hour later there was no sign of abatement when Pike, with commendable husbandly concern for Arlene's welfare, had telephoned the institute to ascertain whether she felt up to driving herself home through the floods or whether she would prefer him to bus or wade along and do it for her. Solicitude for the van itself was not entirely absent from his motivation, but this was not to say that Arlene's comfort and safety were of no account. Pike's intentions were of the purest.

'Car maintenance?' The male voice on the line was peremptory. 'That finished an hour ago. They've all gone.'

'Knocked off early, did they, because of the weather?'

From the far end came a scornful intake of breath. 'We don't let the climate govern us. Your wife's course always ends at nine.'

Pike's stomach gave a kick. 'I see,' he said on a note of

casual enlightenment. 'She'll have left, then. You wouldn't happen to know if she'd any problem with her transport? I was wondering if the rain—'

'I'm afraid I don't keep a record of individual departures. We tend to be quite busy, actually.'

'Might I have a word,' Pike said humbly, 'with the course instructor?'

'He'll have gone, too.'

'My wife hasn't come home yet. I was wondering—'

'Had you thought of contacting the police?'

Slamming down the receiver, Pike pondered briefly before calling Arlene's parents. There was no reply. He made another call to Deirdre, her elder sister, to learn tersely from her husband that she was in the bath and that Arlene had not visited them that evening, nor was she expected. Pike's relationship with his brother-in-law, as with most of Arlene's family, precluded small-talk; he rang off, gave consideration to the idea of contacting the police, decided against it, dialled the number of his immediate neighbours instead.

'Alec? Can you give us the loan of your wagon for half an hour?'

'Van packed up?' Alec Jones, who worked as a joiner at a local timber yard, sounded both sleepy and evasive. Pike guessed that his lumpish wife Pat was in the room with him.

'Could be. Arlene took it to night class, and with all this rain . . . She might be having starting troubles.'

After an interval, Jones said on a note of reluctance, 'If you want to come round, I'll leave the keys in the porch.'

'Thanks, pal. I might need it for an hour or two, okay?'

'Just park it back outside, when you've finished,' Jones said resignedly.

Pike had borrowed his neighbour's Montego saloon before, and enjoyed the feel of it in contrast to the seven-year-old, high-mileage Escort van which he and Arlene used both

as trade workhorse and runabout. Tonight, he was in no
mood to relish the difference. Pursuing the direct route
through the torrent to the institute, he spotted no sign of
catastrophe along the way; no ambulance flashing lights, no
wrecked shopfront with a vehicle hanging out of it. The
streets, in fact, were largely deserted, and on arrival at the
further education centre he found a similar scene. No light
was visible and the car park was empty. Without bothering
even to ring at the main door, he drove off and took a detour
or two in the obscure hope of coming upon the van in one
of several places that Arlene might conceivably have taken
it into her head to visit—her friend Linda's house, for
example, in Pines Close; or her younger brother's current
residence, a marginally upmarket squat in a house behind
the High Street that was scheduled for demolition. In neither
case was his quest rewarded.

Now beginning to be thoroughly alarmed, he took a
broader sweep that carried him the several rain-drenched
miles to Beech Chase. After a three-hour downpour, the
unmade road surface had reverted to a nightmare of pools
and thick mud, through and across which Pike coaxed the
saloon until in the watery beam of his headlamps he was
able to discern the low-slung hulk of his partner's Mercedes
parked in the front driveway of the coach-house with its
prow half-buried in an adjacent shrub. Pulling up opposite,
he lowered the Montego's window and peered out. With a
clearer view, he could now see that the Mercedes was not
the sole occupant of the space available in front of the
coach-house. To its left, almost concealed by a row of
conifers, sat Pike's Escort van.

For long moments he stared at it. He was trying to recall
whether, in a spasm of semi-lunacy, he had asked Arlene to
deliver a message by hand to Somers and then had forgotten
he had done so. On either count, the likelihood was faint to
the point of non-existence. If he had, he wouldn't have

forgotten; and the need, in any case, would never have arisen. If there had been anything for him and his partner to talk about, he had only to have lifted the telephone.

A haven in the storm?

This made no sense, either. From the technical institute, it was further to the coach-house than to the Pikes' home, with the added hazard of the unmade road and its water-troughs. There was no climatic reason for Arlene to have driven there. Pike himself had tried it only as a last resource, on the off-chance that his partner might have some helpful suggestions to offer and even be willing to give moral support by coming out with him in the Montego to join in the search. The notion of finding the van in physical occupation of the front garden had never for an instant occurred to him.

Finally, dousing the car lights, he scrambled out into a fusillade of raindrops and a deep puddle. Cursing, he zipped his leather jacket to the neck and wallowed across the road —it more closely resembled a riverbed—to test the van's door-handles, front and rear. All were locked.

Between the drawn curtains of the main downstairs window of the coach-house, light trickled. The leakage was pencil-slim. Pike hesitated. Presently he returned to the Montego, restarted the engine.

Easing the car along to the side entrance, a distance of twenty yards, he turned into it and followed what was little more than a rutted track, currently awash, for a further thirty yards to the point at which it divided, the left-hand fork leading off to the former parent structure of the property, a turreted and gabled folly built by a retired grocery tycoon with delusions of nobility and now occupied, reputedly, by a reclusive spinster who never ventured beyond its walls and was allowing it to fall irretrievably into decay. To the right of the fork hung a country-style five-barred gate, slimy and fungoid, between timber posts throttled by creeper. On a couple of previous occasions when the Pikes had been entertained by Somers to lunch, this was the route they had taken to their host's rear garden, a lengthy strip of ground of a chiefly arboreal nature, with a cleared patch close to the gate that accommodated a toolshed. Just outside the gate was an area of packed gravel, bonded together by roots, upon which vehicles could be left. Using it to abandon the Montego once more, Pike vaulted the gate.

He landed waist-deep in saturated undergrowth. With more expletives under his breath, he waded soggily to the cinder path that bisected the length of the garden and followed it to the flagstoned patio at the back of the coach-house. The rear window of the living-room was undraped. It was the light from this that had guided Pike from the region of the toolshed. Remaining in shadow, he inched forward until he was in contact with the double-glazing of the sliding door and able to apply his gaze.

Midway down the room, a giant, multiple-cushioned sofa occupied a position diagonal to the side walls, which meant that its back was offered for Pike's inspection while the sprung side was largely obscured. For all this, he could see enough.

More, in fact, than a surplus.

As he watched, momentarily paralysed, a phrase kept beating through his brain. 'Close friends.' How often had he read the words in gossip columns and the like; heard them quoted, with a leer in the voice, on TV and radio bulletins? He had known, of course, what was implied. Detachedly, academically he had known. What had eluded him until now, was a full grasp of the exact degree of proximity involved. For a man who was technically married, Pike had retained a remarkable fund of innocence in respect of matters pertaining to human physical intimacy: his early youth had evaporated in a series of abortive experiments that taught him little, and Arlene had since granted him no opportunity to eliminate his ignorance. Here, for the first time, a picture was being drawn for him, detailed in bold strokes, coloured, varnished.

At one end of the sofa, on the green and purple carpet, lay a small heap of clothing. Most of it was of the feminine variety. The sight of it imbued Pike with a strange, debilitating excitement that, to his mortification, he found not unpleasant. His attention was captured by it, held, welded. Meanwhile the sofa activity hovered on the periphery of his gaze, simultaneously magnetic and repellent. Protected by the Perspex roof of the loggia that covered the patio, he stood there for several minutes until the interior commotion subsided; then he turned and crept back along the path. The rain was easing: it was now no more than a downpour. Swarming over the gate, he reclaimed the Montego, turned it as silently as possible in the confined area, trundled it back to the street and, in a state bordering upon trance, drove it home. Parking it at the kerbside opposite his neighbour's house, he thrust the keys through the letter-flap and retired indoors. He drank a small slug of brandy, undiluted. Then he undressed and went to bed.

When Arlene arrived home, more than an hour later, he pretended to be asleep.

'Not everybody,' remarked Gail, price-marking the final ball of string, 'can be that mad about running a shop. Take me. I'd be useless, cooking supper for my mum and dad, say, seven days of the week. Drive me potty. Not all made the same, are we?'

'More often than not,' Pike said absently, 'we get supper out of a can. Or fetched in from the takeaway. Women don't have to strap themselves to the cooker, these days.'

'I should say not. Ever hear of women's lib?'

Pike had heard of a number of things. He thought about them sometimes, with an underlying sense of uneasiness that verged upon panic. What was it they said and wrote about men who failed to perform but liked to watch? In the months which had succeeded his discovery of Arlene's liaison with Somers, he had asked himself the question with an urgency that was matched by his reluctance to face up to the answer. He couldn't help feeling, in any case, that it was unfair. 'Performance' in this context, by definition, demanded a dual effort. If one of the parties malingered, the other could hardly be condemned for falling down on the job as well. What was he, Pike, supposed to do? Act the savage?

Civilized people avoided such measures. They were content to wait, to bide their time until sanity and fair-mindedness prevailed. This was all he had been doing: soft-pedalling, giving Arlene the chance to come to him in her own way, at her own speed. Refusal to take the initiative had nothing to do with it.

Nevertheless the question declined to go away.

At the same time, there was a balancing factor, a consolation. In the aftermath of his traumatic discovery, Pike came gradually to appreciate that, if Arlene and Somers had something over him, he in turn had something just as potent over them. He possessed, in short, a secret weapon; one that could readily be deployed if ever it were needed. This, by itself, was no bad feeling.

# CHAPTER 4

'Quiet this morning, wasn't it?' observed Gail as she prepared to go for lunch. 'Must be a lot of people away.'

Pike nodded. 'Come July,' he said from the shop window, 'they drop off like flies. All these package tours and suchlike. Trade'll buck up again in September, you'll see.'

From where he stood, he could see along the parade as

far as the sub-post office on the other side of the street. As a result of personal scrutiny for the past ten minutes, he could have informed his young assistant that the number of Chipperford citizens apparently requiring postage stamps had shown no hint of slackening, holiday season or not. The spectacle had filled him with an almost unbearable dejection which he was finding it difficult to disguise. Squaring his shoulders, he returned to the counter.

'No need to hurry back,' he told her, adding a few extra packets of chewing gum to the array in front of the till. 'We're not likely to be trampled in the rush, this afternoon.'

At the doorway, Gail squinted up at the midday sunlight before peeling the cotton back from her forearms, exposing flesh that was browned and rounded, with a hint of freckles. 'Might grab a coat of suntan in the Library Grounds,' she remarked, inspecting the underside of each arm with clinical intensity. 'Back by two-ish, okay?'

'Whenever you like.'

The examination shifted to him. 'You eating here?'

Pike shrugged. 'I may not bother.'

'You should, you know. It's bad for you, going without food all day.'

On impulse he said, 'Where do you generally go?'

'Burger Bar along the street. Or I might get something from the takeaway. I could always fetch you in a Salami Special. Fancy one?'

With decisive movements, Pike switched off and locked the till. 'Seeing it's a nice day, I might as well join you. That's if you've no objection.'

'Me? What d'you take me for? Only thing is, if we're both—'

'To hell with it.' Nudging her through the doorway, Pike turned the sign to read CLOSED, slammed and locked the door, joined her on the pavement. 'If they want serving in the lunch hour, they'll have to wait. I can't be at their beck and call. Burger Bar, then?'

'If you like.' Gail was regarding him in a way he hadn't seen from her before: a kind of curiosity. 'First time I've known you hand things to the competition on a plate.'

'Patels, you mean? They're welcome. There's more to life than profit and loss accounts. Anyway there should be.'

'Try telling that to the Chamber of Commerce. Never throught you had it in you, Marve. You'll be shutting on Mondays, next.'

Pike was a little appalled at himself. What had induced this small burst of rebellion? He was committed now. He couldn't backtrack without losing face. Trailing his assistant into the Burger Bar, he stood aside while she ordered a couple of gigantic bun-and-steak concoctions and coffee in chimney-pot beakers. Reckless behaviour, he admonished himself. A lot of goodwill, painstakingly built up over months and years, could vanish like smoke in this way. Somers, if he found out, would have a legitimate beef. He would be entitled to . . .

For Christ's sake. On any rating of the situation, Pike reflected, his partner hadn't a leg to stand on. He contributed nothing. The reverse, indeed. There he was, sucking the lifeblood from the business; and here was he, Pike, fretting over sixty minutes snatched from slavery. Pursuing Gail to a corner table, he demanded of himself how this mental block had become fixed, implanted, so that the time was imminent when he would be able to see nothing beyond it on either side. He, Pike, was the injured party. Somers was the culprit. Remember that. Keep it clearly in mind.

'Well!' Gail handed him a paper table-napkin with 'BB' stamped across it, and poured low-calorie sweetener into her coffee. 'Makes a change, I must say. Lunch with the Boss.' She turned another of her diligent scrutinies upon him. 'Somethink on your mind, Marve? You're looking sort of . . .'

'Not been sleeping too well,' he explained, launching a gingerly assault upon the squashy rim of his beefburger with his front teeth. 'Tends to catch up with you, after a while.'

'Don't I know.' Small bubbling noises came from her lips as she drew coffee from the chimney-pot. 'It's rotten, stopping awake half the night. Generally means you've somethink niggling at you, like.' She blinked at him. 'Sometimes it can help to tell somebody. Not bottle it up.'

'Everyone has problems.'

'There's different types, though. Some lousier than others.'

Pike regarded her through a shroud of shredded steak and onion fumes. 'How about you, Gail? You got troubles?'

She considered. 'Dad gets on at us, sometimes,' she volunteered. 'Then again, I can't seem to lose weight for more'n a couple of weeks at a time. At the moment we've got men digging the road up at home, laying pipes. So the whole place is a right mess and I have to carry me bike, practically, for the last quarter of a mile. Things like that.'

He gave her a slight smile 'Call them problems?'

'No,' she replied promptly. 'Pinpricks, you might say. Nothink like yours, I don't suppose.'

'I don't, either. Mine have to do with trade.'

She nodded wisely. 'The way it's dropping off, you mean? Funny, that. No special reason for it, as I can lay me finger on. I mean, we flog most things that people—'

'It's not just a question of turnover. There's a separate factor involved.' Pike liked the smack of that phrase. It had a properly unspecific and yet pervasively sinister flavour, committing him to nothing while insinuating volumes. 'An extra dimension, so to speak.' That wasn't a bad one, either. In adversity, his gift of the gab seemed to blossom and flourish. Maybe he should try it on his partner some time.

Gail continued to look sage, although an element of perplexity was discernible behind the mask. 'Profit margins . . . ?' she suggested timidly.

'That comes into it.'

'Still, I mean, we don't mark stuff down a lot, do we? Patels undercut us, most of the time.'

'More capitalization behind 'em, probably.' Pike spoke with glib authority. 'They can afford to make a loss on certain lines for a while.'

'Till they've forced us out of business?'

'They won't do that.'

' 'Course they won't. You get in there, Marve, and fight.'

'I don't mind fighting. In retail, you need to be a scrapper. Only it's not so easy when you've an arm tied behind your back.'

Gail bit meditatively into her beefburger, her attention apparently with the traffic in the street outside. 'The extra dimension, you're talking about?'

'Right.' Pike leaned back to circulate his jaws with an air of mystery. Gail was having none of that.

'So what is it?' she demanded.

'It's something,' he stalled, 'I have to think carefully about. A shade delicate.'

'What's delicate about it?'

'Let's say it concerns . . . relationships as well as commerce.' Pike had a dim suspicion that he might be drifting out of his depth. He made an attempt to veer from the topic. ''Not bad, these, are they? Only they're a mite heavy with the garlic.'

'Eat up. Do you good.' Gail studied him silently for a few moments, before producing her bombshell. 'It's Gareth, isn't it? He's been cooking the books?'

Shock-blasted, he stared back at her. When he had enough wind to speak, he said, 'If I'd known you had your suspicions . . .'

'Me? Suspicions?' She sniffed loudly and swigged some coffee. 'I knew all along. Soon as you did, nearly, I bet. You can't pull one over on me.'

'No, well, you're a smart one, Gail,' he mumbled. 'I've always thought so.' He scratched his scalp. 'Seeing as you knew, why didn't you mention it before?'

'I thought you was just putting up with it, like. Accepting it.'

'No way,' Pike said fervently. 'No *way.*'

'What you going to do about it, then?'

'I'm pondering the alternatives.'

Another good phrase. Pike felt that his vocabulary was standing up well to the battering demands being made upon it lately. Gail, to his chagrin, barely seemed to notice. She snorted.

'He wants seeing off.'

'There are various—'

'He ought to be reported. If he's rooking you, Marvin, that's theft. You could get him shoved in clink.'

'What good would that do?'

Gail's nose went into wrinkles. 'Wouldn't be around any more, would he, to swipe things off you? You'd have a free hand.'

Pike sagged worriedly into his chair. 'Sounds easy, but . . .'

'You can keep books. You've got a diploma, you told me. Who needs Gareth? With him out the way, you might even start showing a profit.'

The faithfulness with which she was echoing his own reflections was uncanny. Pike gazed at her with a new respect, while continuing automatically to prevaricate. 'Not if I'm juggling with figures into the small hours, I wouldn't. I'd be snoring over the till.'

'Fetch Arlene in to help out.'

'Arlene doesn't care about the shop.'

'If it looked like going under, she'd care. It's her bread and butter, remember, besides yours.'

'I'm not so sure of that.'

The words slipped out before he knew they were forming. He hoped Gail hadn't heard them, but she had. She stopped chewing. Her eyes, very alert, were fixed upon his. 'You mean,' she said eventually, 'she's got other irons, like, in the fire?'

Pike winced. 'In a manner of speaking.'

'What irons? What fires?'

'I'd sooner not talk about it, Gail. D'you mind?'

'Yes,' she declared, to his amazement. 'I do mind. You're in trouble, Marvin, and you're telling us about it. You wouldn't be doing that unless you wanted advice. Only I can't give you any if I'm not in the picture, can I? Stands to reason.'

Shoving back his chair, Pike slumped again, gazed unseeingly through the window at a passing bus. 'There's no call,' he muttered, 'for you to be loaded with my problems. As long as—'

'Yes, there is. Up to a point, they're *my* problems. Supposing the shop goes bust? I'm out of a job, aren't I? Besides . . .' She peeped at him across the table. 'I *want* to help. I like you, Marvin. You've been good to me and I don't fancy seeing you miserable. They say it's better if you've someone to talk to. So, go ahead and talk. Where's the harm?'

Pike's defences crumbled.

'You're quite a girl. I never knew you were taking such a . . . Well, okay, brace yourself.' Leaning forward, he planted both elbows on the table and glared downwards at the remnants of beefburger strewn about their plates. 'Here it comes. Arlene's having it away with Gareth. It's been going on for months, and my guess is she knows what he's been up to, into the bargain. So she's not likely to come

riding to *my* assistance, is she, like the Seventh Cavalry?'
He looked up. 'Now you know.'

Gail said calmly. 'I've known all along.'

Late that afternoon, Somers paid a rare visit to the shop.

'Just on my way back,' he explained, 'from fixing a deal
with Mason's. They're giving us top-whack discount on
stationery, selected lines, plus free deliveries for six months.
Worth the trip, huh? Even though it took a hunk out of my
day.'

Completing delivery of a can of Coke to a small boy, Pike
waited until the child was out of the shop before adding the
money carefully to the day's hoard. 'Discount? How much?'

'I told you. The best.'

'Twenty per cent? Twenty-five?'

Somers laughed tolerantly. 'You carry on charming the
customers, Pikey, and I'll look after my side. Take my word
for it, we're getting a bargain. They seem to like me at
Mason's. I lunched with Cranmore and his deputy, and
they were telling me—'

'Welling would give us twenty per cent, if we went to 'em
tomorrow.'

'Welling's products,' Somers returned smoothly, 'are
qualitatively inferior. Also they can be tacky on deliveries.
Relax, my son. This deal will be good for both of us. How's
trade been, today?'

'Much as usual.'

Somers, hands deep in tailored pockets, regarded him
whimsically. 'That's not terribly informative.'

'No? Sorry. It's a habit I must be picking up from somebody.'

Traces of doubt seeped into his partner's survey. 'You
feeling all right?'

'I'm fine, in myself.' Pike began slapping the early evening
newspapers into a neater stack to make way for the later

edition, due any moment. 'Where you off to now?' he inquired. 'Home, to cook the books?'

'That's it.' Somers took it in jocular spirit. 'The weekly camouflage operation, anti-Revenue division.' He turned to examine the shop's interior. 'Where's young Gail? Knocked off early?'

'Some of us put in a full day.' The girl had appeared suddenly from the stockroom. Grime streaked the front of her blouse, and a hank of hair hung over her nose. 'Come to lend us a hand, like?' She dumped a carton of adhesive tubes on the counter. 'There's half a dozen more this size to come through, if you're feeling energetic.'

'What I'm feeling,' Somers replied with dignity, 'is a touch of dyspepsia from curried chicken.' He reached out to pat her shoulder as she passed him, but was eluded. 'You're doing such a first-rate job, Gail, I wouldn't dream of interfering. Anyway it's good for your figure. All that bending and stretching.'

'You should know about figures.' Stalking back to the stockroom, she clashed the door behind her.

Somers watched her go. 'Quite a little mouse, she used to be,' he said mildly. 'Why do I get the impression she's just been fed raw meat?'

'Could be she's feeling overworked.'

'Exploited, you mean?'

'She does a lot of heavy lifting.'

Mirth trumpeted from Somers. 'If you're afraid she's heading for a slipped disc, why not put her on light duties? We can't afford to shell out on industrial injuries.'

'Someone has to cope with the heavy stuff.'

'Behave like a gentleman, Pikey, even if your performance is rusty. Take the manual chores over from the young lady.'

Pike eyed him stonily. 'Both of us do our share, it might surprise you to learn.'

'At a price, you could always hire a fork-lift truck.'

'An extra pair of hands now and then would do nicely.'

The smile stayed riveted to Somers's cheeks. 'Wouldn't be dropping a broad hint, Pikey, would you, by any chance?'

'I'm not dropping any kind of a hint. I'm giving it to you straight. We could use a bit of grafting from somebody else with an interest in the business. I don't reckon that's so much to ask.'

Rocking lazily from toes to heels, Somers produced a brief whistling noise through his front teeth. 'Do I ask you to help run over the accounts?'

'No. But I'm willing.'

'Armed with your Diploma in book-keeping.' Somers said it half-waggishly, in the manner of a parent not displeased with the effort made by his offspring while knowingly sceptical of the result. He patted his partner's arm. 'As I said, Pikey, we need you up front. You're the public relations artist, the guy who—'

'Public? They're getting a bit thin on the ground, these days.' Pike retreated out of range of the other's pawing fingers. 'Not too crazy about our prices, I reckon. If we could drop a percentage of 'em, we might get somewhere.'

Somers wagged his head. 'Not on. We're nudging break-even point, as it is.'

'With all these discounts you keep getting?'

'Discounts don't achieve miracles. Like most firms, we're having to run to stand still.'

'*I'm* running,' Pike said nastily. 'Gail and me, we're both at the double. What pace d'you reckon you're keeping up?'

Somers looked hurt. 'There's gratitude. What do you think I've been doing all week? Sitting on my backside, ruling lines in a ledger?'

'I'm quite sure you've been busy. What I'm saying is,

where's the benefit to us of all this hard work? I don't seem to be seeing any.'

'You get the stock, don't you? Fixed price, on time, no hassle over deliveries . . .'

'Except we're not getting enough.'

'Not enough?'

'Supplies,' Pike said clearly, lifting his chin, 'seem to be short. We keep running out of things when we shouldn't. We're not flogging the stuff, Gail and me, to that extent. What happens to it?'

Their gazes met, locked. Somers said with a confident air, 'Obviously you're doing better than you think. You must be selling it. Otherwise it wouldn't keep vanishing, would it?'

'Unless it was never here in the first place.'

'I don't follow.'

'I mean,' said Pike, slowly and distinctly, 'unless the quantities you order aren't reaching our stockroom. Getting diverted, somehow.'

'How would that be possible?'

'You tell me.'

Somers stared at him with a puckered forehead. He seemed on the point of saying something when a woman entered the shop and Pike moved along to attend to her. Alerted by the doorbell, Gail re-emerged from the back, saw that matters were in hand, lobbed Somers a frosty glance and turned to immure herself again. He took a pace or two in pursuit.

'Have you been insinuating things to my partner?'

'Me? I don't deal in insinuations, I'll have you know. Anything I might think, I come straight out with, don't you worry.'

'And what is it you've been coming straight out with, just lately?'

'Give us a couple of hours,' she said haughtily, 'and I'll

make you out a list. Have to excuse us for now. Bit pushed, you know.' Marching back to the stockroom, she re-closed the door with a thump.

The woman customer left the shop. Returning to the counter, Somers supported himself upon it with an elbow and submitted Pike to a hard, brooding inspection. Refilling the space left by the woman's purchase of three slabs of fruit-and-nut chocolate, Pike feigned oblivion of his partner's presence. Somers rapped the glass surface of the counter ringingly with his fingertips.

'Shall I tell you something? I don't *think* I care too much for what I've just been hearing.'

'When are you likely to decide?'

Somers flushed heavily. 'Skip the wisecracks, Marvin. You're not on stage now. Those bit parts you used to play at school went to your head, if you ask me. You just want to be a comedian.'

'At least it's an honest profession.'

'And while you're at it, you might avoid the insinuations as well. Being a tolerant sort of a guy, I'm prepared on this occasion to—'

'If you're not feeling inclined to lend a hand with the humping, Gareth, you might try making some space in front of the counter. We're a bit cluttered.'

Pike's partner walked slowly to the door. With fingers on the pull-handle, he paused and turned.

'Maybe we should have a serious talk, Marvin, you and I. My place, tomorrow night?'

'As long as you're not entertaining anyone else. Arlene has plans, I believe, for washing her hair. So, no problem where she's concerned.'

Somers gave him another hard look.

Dabbing at buttons, Pike restored the till register electronically to zero. 'I'll be along,' he said, without glancing up. 'Eight-thirty or thereabouts. Save us a place on the sofa.'

# CHAPTER 5

Unexpectedly, that evening, Arlene arrived home earlier than usual from 'night class'.

Pike was sprawled in his special chair, the teak-framed one with a raked backrest and outsize castors that enabled it to be trundled around like a tea-trolley. He had picked it up for a song from a dealer in second-hand household rarities and, despite or perhaps in defiance of Arlene's disapproval of the piece as an item of living-room furniture, had cherished and monopolized it ever since. He had often nursed a secret fear that he would return home one day to find that Arlene had pitched it out for collection by the town's dustmen. So far she hadn't. There were lengths, it appeared, to which even disgruntled wives were not prepared to go. Except possibly when pushed to the limit.

When Arlene came in, Pike was watching a TV comedy show which, at the moment of her entry, had abandoned straight humour in favour of a 'dance' routine by five under-clad females of a description that in less enlightened times would have given rise to questions in Parliament. Pike, to do him justice, hadn't chosen to watch it. The show had followed the news bulletin, and he had simply felt too flaked out to heave himself clear of the chair's cushions to switch over or switch off. Arlene's initial comment was accordingly hard to take.

'So this is the kind of garbage you look in at, whenever I'm out.'

'Poke it off, if you want. I'm not interested.'

'No. I can see that.'

Behind the mockery, could he detect a trace of wariness?

Pike glanced up at her. Instead of doing as he had suggested, she stood observing the feline antics on screen while slowly removing, button by button like an amateur stripper, the vivid green polyester cardigan she had worn to the institute over her blouse and cream cotton trousers. The faintest smear of what looked like engine oil decorated the side of her left temple, just below the hairline. To Pike, it almost gave the impression of having been applied subtly, on purpose. He decided upon attack.

'Got yourself nicely messed up, I see.'

Her hand went instantly to the spot. 'It's a mucky course,' she said with studied vagueness, tossing the cardigan on to an arm of her own, more conventional chair, then stepping back to give the screen caperers another vetting. 'If you're still looking,' she added, less astringently, 'I'll leave it on while I make the ReadyWhip. Want some?'

'Don't mind.' A bedtime liking for hot malted milk was one of the rare things they had in common. Now that Pike thought about, there was virtually nothing else. Books? Newspapers? Television? On any subject you cared to mention, their tastes diverged. Arlene enjoyed biographies of dead royalty, tabloid Press features on media personalities, and televized travel documentaries. Pike, when he had time to read, which was seldom, devoured war sagas and skimmed the newspaper columns for items about the City and the Welfare State, on both of which topics he held firm and less than indulgent views; while his viewing energies were expended chiefly upon screen transmutations of the classics. Arlene liked to watch the tennis. Possessing not the slightest aptitude for anything of a physical nature, except moving merchandise around a shop, Pike had no corresponding urge to watch others flexing sinew. It was the same with everything. At no point did they come together. When they did communicate verbally, it tended to be exclusively on the matters of household requirements and financial stringency. This made for occasional liveliness, but hardly constituted a bond.

Retiring to the kitchen, Arlene rattled utensils about. By the exertion of considerable effort, Pike got himself across to the TV set and dismissed the dancers, whose orgasmic writhings had by now overstepped the borderline between eroticism and the purely grotesque; although this was not how Pike expressed it to himself. He merely opined that they were 'coming it a bit strong'. Was he a prude? He had no idea. There were times when he strongly suspected that he might be: others when the hypothesis seemed to stand itself on its head. Where Arlene, for instance, was concerned . . .

His observance of her and Somers in the middle of manœuvres had lasted some while, and ever since that traumatic occasion he had harboured the uneasy feeling that an element of semi-enjoyment had not been too distant from his reactions. What could it mean? Was he a psychological mess, a psychopath in the making? Human behaviour under stress was a sphere in which Pike took a solemn, uneducated interest and was apt to consult manuals about it when he had the chance.

At this moment, there were other things to do. Instead of returning to his teak chair, he sat up at the table by the drawn curtains and reopened the cardboard folder that he had left on the cloth.

Extracting a balance-sheet, he hung close-work spectacles on his nose and ears and launched a narrow-eyed survey of the figures. He was thus engaged when Arlene bore in a tray decked with two brimming porcelain mugs and a dish of assorted biscuits which she planted at his elbow.

'Why didn't you start that earlier, instead of watching the box?'

'Too fagged,' he said briefly.

'What's made *you* so tired?' Her tone suggested that in

anyone else fatigue was permissible; in Pike's case it was on
the proscribed list.

'Could be a hard day's graft.' His own tone remained
abstracted. An aura of faint bafflement emanated from
Arlene's stance. Taking her ReadyWhip to the armchair,
she perched on its cushioned back and took a couple of
exploratory sips, watching him.

'Is it getting on top of you?'

He looked up. 'Is what?'

'The shop. The business. Would you sooner be doing
something else?'

'Like what?'

She wriggled her shoulders. 'Some office job. Accountancy? You've got this fantastic diploma, after all. Why not
make some use of it?'

Pike shifted himself in the chair to face her. 'What d'you
reckon I'm doing, right now?'

She looked nonplussed. 'I was just asking. It's your
decision.'

'What is?'

'Whether to keep on with the shop or not.'

'Yours as much as mine, I should hope.'

'And Gareth's.'

'Ah yes. Gareth. Mustn't overlook him.'

Taking a hasty gulp from her mug, she studied him
through a mantle of eyelashes. Tonight (Pike had to admit
it) she looked a complete knockout. Love, they said, did
marvels for a woman's appearance. Did straightforward lust
have the same effect?

'You talk,' said Arlene, 'as if you *were* overlooking him.'

Laying down the balance-sheet, Pike leaned back to eye
the ceiling. 'No. Can't say I was. We're in partnership,
aren't we? No turning a blind eye to that.'

'You're in a funny mood tonight.'

'How d'you make that out?'

'I thought you and Gareth were buddies. Now you're talking as if you'd taken a dislike to him.'

'Am I?

'You get on all right, don't you? The two of you?'

'I don't get much of a chance to find out. We hardly see each other.'

'You saw him just this aft . . .' Arlene stopped, buried her face in the mug. Emerging, she added, 'You see enough of him to rate him as a business partner, I'd have thought.'

'Oh, I've assessed him there, all right.'

'You shouldn't jump to conclusions. It's dangerous.'

'What conclusions?'

'About Gareth.'

'What makes you think I have?'

'I don't know anything about it,' Arlene said irritably. 'I'm just going by your tone of voice.'

Pike meditated. 'Is that all?' he inquired presently.

'Is what all?'

'My tone of voice. Sure you've not been having a cosy little debate about the set-up, you and Gareth, behind my back?'

'Don't be so stupid.'

'I'm trying not to be. I'm trying to be a step ahead, for once. You mentioned just now about jumping to conclusions.' Pike lifted his chin at her. 'You're the one doing that, I reckon.'

Arlene lowered her mug. 'What are you getting at, might I ask?'

'Telling me I saw Gareth this afternoon. I did, as it happens. But how did you know, my love? I don't remember telling you.'

There was a pause. 'If you must know,' Arlene said finally, 'Gareth phoned me afterwards.'

'Oh, he did? This a habit of his?'

'No. He was a bit upset, that's all. Said you'd had a

quarrel. He wanted to talk to someone about it.'

'I don't know,' Pike said musingly, 'as I'd call it a *quarrel*. An Exchange of Views.'

'That's not the way he described it. He said you'd flung all sorts of veiled accusations.'

'While he kept a dignified silence?'

'There wasn't any point, he said, trying to answer them at the time. He thought it was best to discuss it later, when you'd both simmered down.'

'Maybe he hasn't *got* any answers.'

'If that's the way you feel, there doesn't seem much point in getting together.'

'You might be right,' Pike conceded graciously. 'I'm probably too prejudiced to give him a fair hearing. Why don't you pop over and see him for me?'

'Pop over where?'

'His house. That's where we arranged to talk. You know where his house is, don't you?'

'It's more than a year since you took me there. I doubt if I could—'

'Since I took you there . . . certainly.' Despite his outward appearance of calm, Pike's heartbeat was lurching like a landlubber at sea in a storm. 'That's not the last time you went, though, surely? I mean, we're friends of Gareth. You just said so.'

'Friendship doesn't necessarily mean visiting terms.' Arlene's voice, her manner, her entire personality had tightened up. 'I've enough to do with my time. Why would I want to drag right over there?'

'You know something, love? That's exactly the question I've been asking myself.'

The silence within the room became hazardous. Only a flicker of a gesture was needed to launch heavy gunfire. Arlene seemed to be pondering. Without watching her, Pike was acutely aware of every shade of expression that passed

across her face, the least alteration in her body-posture; so
that he was not startled when she rose from the chair-back,
approached him menacingly and took up a new position
stiff-spined against the curtain, glaring down at him from
high altitude. Her jaw, he noticed, had undergone the slight
dislocation that had once afflicted it at school when she was
charged, justly, with causing a disturbance in the play-
ground. On that occasion she had fast-talked herself out of
trouble and transferred the blame to somebody else, into
the bargain. Ever since then, Pike had been a grudging
admirer of her performance under pressure.

'Are you implying what I think you're implying? You
must be out of your mind.'

'I've said nothing yet. If you really—'

'Pardon me, you've said a bundle. You've as good as
accused me of having some big thing going with Gareth—
right?'

'You said it, not me.'

'You bet I said it. You haven't the spunk, yourself. You
snivelling little coward. All you can do is insinuate. First
Gareth, now me. You're afraid to come right out with
anything. What's the matter, sonny? Frightened of getting
hurt?'

Pike looked up at her. 'If it makes you feel any better, I
don't mind coming out with it. How long d'you plan to keep
it up, you and him?'

He was by now sufficiently familiar with her ways to detect
a lessening—slight but definite—of her self-assurance, a
slackening of the coiled spring she had made of herself.
Abruptly, Arlene was treading shakier ground. By launching
an immediate assault, she had thought to disarm him, as
had happened so often before; the unexpected counter-
punch had got through to graze her chin.

'What makes you think I've been seeing him?'

Pike could have laughed. In the normal way, Arlene

would neatly have sidestepped such a verbal pitfall. The fact that she had allowed herself to give voice to it was a sure sign of momentary uncertainty. Committed now, he leapt in to follow up.

'What makes me think so?' He pointed to his eyes. 'See these? Twenty-twenty vision, they've got. They tell me all I want to know.'

Arlene's eyebrows came together. 'What's that supposed to mean?'

'It means I'm not blind, that's what. I can follow the action when it's played through for me.'

'Action?' she repeated steadily.

Pike's tongue strode on, running away with him. 'The Sofa Stakes. Fond of sofas, aren't you, Arlene? Especially big, soft ones, with nice fat cushions. Especially when there's good company. Mind you, I'd feel inclined to take a few precautions, myself. If it was privacy I was after, that is. For a start, I'd pull the curtains across the patio doors. Never know, do you, who might be watching?'

The face staring down at him had whitened as he was speaking. As he stopped, the colour began racing back, twice as rampant as before: her lips trembled, but not because of apprehension. This time it was fury, loathing, disbelief. With a few words, Pike had caused this. He felt a little awed.

Her own words, when they came, commenced with deceptive mildness. 'You know, Marvin, there's one thing I was always convinced of, where you're concerned.'

'Oh yes? And what's that?'

'You'd sooner be watching than doing. It's the one thing you're good at.'

'Some of us aren't given the chance to do much else.'

'Oh, I see. It's everybody else's fault. That figures. When you can't justify yourself, blame the umpire. You nasty little self-centred, self-seeking—'

'I don't need to blame umpires, Arlene, or anyone else. Apart from you.'

'Careful, sweetie. I might be tempted to hit back.'

'Try it.'

'I don't have to try. The whole thing speaks for itself.'

'I don't know what you're on about.'

'No? Just think about it. If a girl can't get what she wants in one direction, she's going to head off in the other, right? Even you should see that.'

Pike rose, gripping the table-edge. 'Watch what you're saying, Arlene. Just . . . watch it, that's all.'

'You're forgetting something. I don't have to watch. I'm one of life's doers—remember? I like to *perform*.' She made the word steel-tipped, dipped in poison. 'You're the one, my lad, with a practical problem. And I'm not talking about the retail trade, though heaven knows you don't exactly shine in that department, from what I hear. I'm talking about the things that really interest a woman. Want to keep listening?'

'Steady on.' Pike heard the words faintly, from a distance. He wasn't sure whether it was he who had uttered them.

'Typical!' She had the whip hand now. She knew it: she was exultant. 'You can't even keep up a good squabble. Soon as the chips are down, you start whining. You're watered milk. Small wonder if I go elsewhere for entertainment. Any other man would have reacted by now. *Done* something. Not you. Anything for a quiet life. If I was being raped in that corner, I don't believe you'd lift a finger to help. You're a long thin streak of nothing, you know that? You wouldn't know how to—'

'Shut up! Shut *up*!'

'Why should I? You're the one started this. Now you can damn well listen. It's time you heard a few home truths. My God, how did I ever marry a nothing like you? I must

have been insane. You talked me into it. "In ten years I'll
be a millionaire" . . . Whoopee! I believed you. For a few
weeks I actually thought you meant what you said. That
was before I found out all the other minus things about
you. Next to Gareth, you're vermin. You want crushing
underfoot. No, you're worse than a rat. Male rats at least
do things to female rats. You? You just leave it to somebody
else. Someone who's twenty times the man you'll ever be.
Like to hear a few details about Gareth? Physical details?
Stand by, here they come. In the first place . . .'

Pike closed his eyes. He could hear, faintly, Arlene's voice
raving on, but the worst of it was starting to be drowned
out by rival noises whose source he couldn't immediately
identify. Weird popping sounds. They seemed to come from
inside his own ears, deep inside his own head. And although
his eyes were shut, he could still see Arlene's face, directly
ahead of him, with the lips writhing as the toxin poured out.
Perhaps, by reaching out, he could arrest the flow. It was
worth a try.

His fingers closed upon soft, warm flesh.

Through the tumult inside his eardrums, he picked up a
giggle. He forced his eyes to reopen, to focus. He was right.
Arlene was yielding to mirth. It made no sense. The laugh,
surely, was on her? The reality must be driven home, otherwise he would be in the absurd position of holding the
whip hand and yet being belaboured sneakily from behind.
Intolerable.

Presently the giggling stopped. This was a vast relief.
The room was now silent, totally free of aural distraction.
Anxious to keep it that way, he maintained pressure. Life
had taught him at least one lesson: never relax too soon.
The flesh between his hands was gaining weight, forcing
down his arms, making him buckle at the knees. An odd
effect; but the silence was continuing and this was all that
mattered. He dreaded a resumption. The giggle or the words

—either would have been insupportable. To prevent it, he was willing to stay there for an hour, for a day, doing what was necessary.

Presently, however, the stillness was again disrupted.

Only this time it wasn't so bad. Instead of a giggle, a gurgle. Or was it a kind of choking? Either way, he preferred it to its predecessor. Even so, the absolute silence was best of all. The weight was dragging him down: dimly he had the impression that he was on his knees. But the noise had finally surrendered.

# CHAPTER 6

Somers sounded sleepy.

'Who? Marvin! What time of night do you call this?'

'I know it's late,' said Pike, 'but I'm worried about Arlene. Is she with you?'

'With *me*?' His partner's tone of amazement would have duped a High Court judge. 'What gave you that idea?'

'It was just a hope, really. I've tried everywhere else. You've not seen her tonight, then?'

'Is she missing?'

'She went outside a couple of hours ago. Just to check the oil levels on the van, she said. She's not been back since, and there's no sign of her anywhere.'

'Tried the neighbours?' asked Somers, after a pause.

'They've not seen or heard from her.'

'Family, then. Her parents? Any of the—'

'She didn't go to any of them.'

'I still don't understand why you thought she might be here. Had you been fighting?'

'Fighting? Why should we have been?'

'Married couples,' observed Somers, patiently ironic,

'have been known to clash, on occasion. If you two have immunity to the disease, great—only it still doesn't explain where Arlene's got to. You've searched the van?'

'Taken it apart, nearly.'

'Have the oil levels been topped up?'

'No idea. I don't know what they were like before. She used the van earlier on, see, to get to the institute for her maintenance class. When she got back, we both had a bit of supper and then she said she was going outside to see what needed doing. That's the last I saw of her.'

Another silence ticked past at Somers's end. 'Has she done anything like this before? I mean, does she make a habit of—'

'She's quite often come in late from night class. That's different. This time, she was supposed to be just nipping outside for ten minutes. That's what I don't like.'

'I see your point. Where's the van kept?'

'Round the back, up the alleyway. There's a shed we use sometimes, but mainly we leave it in front of the doors. Saves opening up each time.'

'So, if she was checking oil levels, how would Arlene manage for light?'

'She takes a flashlamp.' Pike waited a moment. 'Thanks anyway, Gareth. I'll ring off now, have another scout around. See you.'

'Wait a bit. About tomorrow, Pikey.'

'Tomorrow?'

'Our rendezvous. Our little chat.'

'Forget it. I spoke out of turn. Scrub the meeting.'

'Why not come anyhow, and bring Arlene? Social occasion. You've not been here for a while.'

'That's true,' said Pike. 'I haven't.'

'It's a date, then.'

'What if Arlene's not back?'

'She'll be back,' Somers said confidently. 'People like her

don't vanish for no reason. She'll show up within the next hour or two, or I'm a Chinaman. If not . . .'

'Yes? What do I do then?'

'Call the cops, explain the position. If any kind of . . . incident's been reported, they'll know. They might suggest—'

'Incident?'

'You know. A minor mugging, something of that nature. Arlene could have had something stolen off her while she was working on the van, and taken off in hot pursuit. Which could explain why she's been gone so long.'

'I guess that's possible.'

'If so, you'll get the full story, the works, when she finally storms back.'

'But what if the mugger did her over? Left her lying somewhere?'

'Curb your imagination, old son, that's my advice. I doubt if there *was* a mugger. Talk to the police. They'll know what to do for the best.'

'If you think so. 'Bye now.'

Cradling the receiver, Pike stood gazing down at the instrument, his brows arched in concentration, before giving his body a shake and transporting it back to the table by the curtains. The twin mugs, each containing a quantity of cold and stagnant ReadyWhip, stood side by side on the cloth. Picking them up, he took them through to the tiny kitchen at the back, rinsed and dried them, hung them on their hooks. Keeping the tap running, he splashed his neck, face and forearms and towelled off vigorously, creating a tangle of hair which he restored to order with his comb, paying particular heed to the line of the parting. Having eyed his reflection in the wall-glass from several angles, he applied lacqueur spray. Then he returned to the living-room.

Raising the hem of the tablecloth, he crouched to re-examine Arlene.

She was in the same position, crumpled between the rear legs of the table, hard up against the wall below the curtains. With legs and arms entwined, she looked rather like a prawn. Apprehensive of an icy shock, he hesitated to touch her. When he nerved himself to do it, the warmth of the skin surprised him. After a day of July sunshine, the room was still close. And it was less than two hours, he reminded himself, since it had happened.

So far, his brain was continuing to operate serviceably.

The call to Somers had been the last of a series. Covering tracks, he had concluded, was child's play. It was hard to understand how so many contrived to make such a botch of the procedure. Panic. This had to be the explanation. A misting of judgement.

Which was precisely what Pike aimed to avoid. While the elimination of Arlene had never been top of his priorities, now that it had occurred he was damned if he was going to cast aside any potential benefits for the sake of a fit of the vapours. A true emergency, he was gratified to discover, seemed to bring out the best in him. For once in his life, Pike was having to marshal events rather than be buffeted by them, and he was finding in the experience a strange exhilaration.

Just the same, touching a lifeless torso was not his first choice of enjoyable pastimes. Hastily withdrawing his finger-tips, he remained in a crouch while running fresh data through the computer that had usurped the space previously monopolized by brain tissue—inferior material, as he now acknowledged. High on the list of imponderables was the present behaviour of Somers. What would he be doing, at this instant? How strong was his involvement with Arlene? As a result of Pike's call, what action would he be taking?

The computer came up with the answer. Somers would retire peacefully to bed. News of Arlene's absence for an hour or two would affect him not at all. Why should it?

Obviously the pair of them had been in touch that evening; had arranged, in view of Pike's stated attitude, not to see one another, to cool it for a night; hence Arlene's early arrival home. If he gave any thought to the matter, Somers would ascribe Arlene's disappearance to a fit of restlessness induced by their temporary separation. He might wait for a while by the phone, in case she contacted him. More likely, however, he would go to bed, and sleep soundly.

Either way, Pike's purpose would be admirably served.

Satisfied, he withdrew himself from beneath the table and straightened up. The time was eleven-fifty. He was about to unhook his thin leather jacket from the coat-hanger when the front doorbell shrilled.

In the act of emerging, he had disarranged the leading corner of the tablecloth. Replacing it swiftly, he stood back to assess its efficacy as a screen. Then he went to the street door.

His neighbour, Alec Jones, stood in the porch in his shirtsleeves. 'Before we lock up for the night,' he explained, 'Pat said I should come round and ask after Arlene. She back yet?'

'No sign.' Pike drew an arm across his forehead in a wearily agitated gesture. 'I've been half the night on the blower. Come in a minute.'

Jones looked a shade hunted. 'Can't stop,' he muttered, taking a tentative step into the passage. 'Pat's by herself with the door off the latch. She's not with any of her family, then?'

'Arlene? If she is, they're staying clammed up about it.' Pike puffed his cheeks. 'Time for a quick one? I need something, myself.'

Jones sneaked a glance at his watch. 'It'll have to be *bloody* quick.' He trailed Pike into the living-room. 'Pat'll stir things up if I leave her too long. She reckons nobody's safe in their . . .'

Thinking better of the remark, he placed it in cold storage and accepted a can of mild ale. He poured some of the contents hurriedly down his throat. 'How long's she been gone, now?' Vaguely he nodded in the direction of Arlene's armchair, still bearing the green cardigan.

Pike consulted his own wrist. 'She went out before ten. So it's two hours, close enough.'

'I've just had a glance at the van,' Jones informed him, squinting at the table on which Pike's cardboard folder remained on display. 'Can't see she'd been doing anything to it. Doors all locked.'

Wandering across to the table, Pike stood in front of it while shuffling the loose balance-sheets into order and stowing them back inside the folder. Turning with it clasped to his chest, he stared broodingly at the carpet. 'If she'd been working on it . . .' He looked up. 'There'd be traces, wouldn't there? If she'd been . . . interrupted, I mean. Rags. Oil cans. Junk like that. Don't you reckon?'

Jones, a weedy, youngish man with thin sandy hair, facial freckles amounting almost to a disfigurement, and prominent purple veins on both arms, nodded owlishly. 'You're right. Then again, if she *wasn't* disturbed . . .'

Again he reflected. 'To my way of thinking,' he resumed, 'either she never started the job or else she finished off and then went away somewhere of her own accord. That's how it looks to me.'

Pike planted his own ale-can on the table. 'Tell you what. She's been behaving sort of restless for a while, now. Can't seem to settle, know what I mean? She's not said anything to Pat?'

Jones looked furtive. 'Not as I know of.' He came forward to dump his empty can next to Pike's. 'How about the Fuzz? Called 'em yet?'

'Thought I'd leave it a bit. See if she shows up.' Pike stayed where he was, the backs of his knees brushing the overhang of the tablecloth. Having loitered briefly, eyeing the curtains as though memorizing their colour, Jones swung about.

'I wouldn't hang about too long. Like us to give 'em a bell? Won't take a sec. If you don't feel like ringing yourself.'

'Don't bother, thanks. I'll give it till one. Nice of you to look in, Alec. Appreciate it. You get back to Pat.'

Retreating with alacrity along the passage, Jones turned at the door. 'Arlene's been acting jumpy, you reckon?'

'Not jumpy. I wouldn't call it that. More like . . . dreamy. As if she'd something on her mind. Hard to describe. Dare say I was imagining it.'

'Never know, do we, what they're really thinking?' Jones confided, man to man. 'I'll be off, then. We'll be in touch in the morning.'

'She's sure to be back by then.'

'You bet.'

Pike waited until his neighbour had cleared the porch before shutting the door, switching off the passage light. Back in the living-room, he stood irresolute for a few seconds with his back to the dresser, staring across the room at the triangle of cloth hanging from the table-edge. Suddenly he shuddered.

Taking a couple of deep breaths, he dropped to hands and knees and crawled back under the shroud.


## CHAPTER 7

It was not until the van was bouncing along the deserted, lamplit main road skirting the town centre that some of the tension began to drain from Pike's muscles.

That part was over. A bad part, although worse was guaranteed to come. For the moment, he refused to think ahead in detail. One step at a time. It was therapeutic simply to be on the move, making for somewhere.

The transmission of Arlene from house to vehicle had consumed a sticky ten minutes. From kitchen door to back yard, all the way to the gate in the fence, out into the stony rear access to the all-purpose sheds . . . every step had been the ascent of Everest, a lifetime's effort packed into micro-seconds. At any moment he had expected lights to blaze out, voices to boom: a chorus of attention. Nothing of the kind had occurred, and he was relieved and grateful, but sapped in nerve and strength.

The actual burden of Arlene's body had presented no problem. Although rounded, she was of less than average height and small-boned: some of the packing cases which Pike handled at the shop were heavier. Thin as he was, Pike was wiry, and practice had taught him how to lift. Bend at the knees, keep a straight spine. Tackled correctly, manual elevation was a doddle.

What had surprised him was the lack of stiffening of the body. Rigor mortis, he had always vaguely supposed, was likely to set in within minutes. Far from this, however, Arlene had proved more pliant in death than she ever was, alive. Logistically, the transport operation had gone more smoothly than he could have dared to hope.

Before celebrations were in order, none the less, there remained a great deal more to be done.

Pike reminded himself sternly of this as he negotiated the roundabout that took him on to the ring road which encircled the town. Traffic-free, apart from a heavy goods vehicle keeping steadily ahead of him, it curved gently for a mile until, at the next roundabout, he turned off to follow a minor road to the residential fringes. For the rest of the journey, he had the route to himself.

Since Pike's previous visit, the unmade street in which his partner's house was situated had been earmarked by the local authority as the site for a new water main. It was now in a state of upheaval. Amid the gloom, mechanical excavators stood ghostly between stacked pipe sections and hillocks of hardcore, comprising a hazard which held most of Pike's attention as he steered between the obstructions with dipped headlamps. The mere notion of piling up the van made his heart stop. What if it overturned? What if . . .

With a headshake, he made himself concentrate, drive on cautiously past the coach-house (in darkness) as far as the side entrance. The pipe-laying had yet to reach this point. Turning the van in, he bucked it over the dried and hardened ruts to the compacted area at the fork, where he braked to a halt with the front bumper close up to the gate. He did this in almost total darkness, having doused the headlamps at the mouth of the track. When he switched off the motor, the deathly nocturnal quiet of the neighbourhood was like a sharp blow in the face. What sort of a racket had he created during the final thirty yards? For a few moments he remained seated tautly at the wheel, listening, peering. At last, forcing himself out of the van, he crept round to the rear and opened the nearside door.

Of Arlene, at first, there was no sign. For the fourth or fifth time that night, his heart stopped: then he remembered the ruts and tugged open the offside door. Sure enough, she had been pitched across the loading area to finish in a huddle against the wheel-arch. Clambering inside, he knelt, took a breath, braced his spine and scooped her up.

Back outside, he altered his grip to sling her, fireman's lift fashion, across his left shoulder while he grappled with the gate fastener, a metal hoop that came down over the post. It lifted readily; but when had the gate last been opened? Inclining the combined weight of himself and his

burden against the five-barred barrier, he stumbled a little
as it yielded and drifted back.

Too late, he scented danger. Gaining momentum, the
gate swung out of his reach, scythed through ninety degrees
and struck what was presumably an arresting stake at the
foot of a nearby bush, producing a 'thwack!' that turned
his stomach. Rigid, he stared uselessly into the blackness,
listening once more.

Away to his right, the indistinct mass that was the coach-
house, faintly silhouetted by the light from the street lamps
beyond, remained inert. Presently, able to re-stock his lungs,
Pike trudged through the opening and, keeping with some
difficulty to the cinder path, turned left towards the end
boundary of the garden. It consisted of stake-and-wire fenc-
ing, backed by a riot of thorn hedge and rhododendrons,
with a weed-infested expanse to the fore. Here, he lowered
Arlene to ground level. For all his caution, she landed with
an unpleasant smack, like a doll dropped upon a nursery
floor.

Returning to the garden shed alongside the gateway, he
tested the door. As he had hoped, it opened at a touch.
Inside, he groped about until his fingertips located a shovel
suspended from a rafter. Lifting it down, he took it with him
back to the cattle-fencing.

The choice of a suitable spot exercised him for some
minutes. The one he really fancied proved to be riddled
with tree-roots, impossible to penetrate. The next best lay
between a pair of rusting conifers and behind a shrub:
the space was limited but, Pike estimated, just sufficient.
Making a start, he found to his relief that the roots had not
extended this far, and furthermore that beneath the top
layer of mulch lay a subsoil of loam, easy to dig into. Taking
a couple of deep breaths, he set to work.

Pausing twenty minutes later to rest, he aimed a critical,
night-adjusted eye at the outline of the trench. The dimen-

sions looked about right. It needed to be deeper . . . though not too deep. Flexing his arm-muscles, he got down to it again.

After another half-hour he was satisfied. Returning to Arlene, he hauled her across, straightened her out, lined her up. A few inches short. He dug out another foot or so at one end, toiling at a still more feverish pace, with frequent glances in the direction of the coach-house. It remained unlit. There was no hint of movement anywhere, and yet he had a powerful sense of being under surveillance. Once or twice he wheeled sharply, only to encounter nothing. The pumping of his heart as finally he threw the shovel aside was due only partly to physical exertion. Adopting a position in line with Arlene's midriff, he knelt, placed the palm of each hand against her and executed a quick heave.

With an obedience she had never shown him in life, she toppled over the lip of subsoil to alight on the bed of the trench, face-down. He was relieved about that. Snatching up the shovel again, he covered her with mulch from end to end, trampled it down, added more. When the surface was roughly even, he stood back and surveyed the patch.

Good enough. He returned the shovel to the shed. On re-emergence, he turned to the right this time, making for the house.

By the time he had selected what seemed to him an appropriate spot on the pathway, Pike's hands were shaking uncontrollably. He had taken more than he could bear. Trying to move quickly, he felt incapable of doing more than drag himself along while time hurtled by, outstripping his efforts, mocking him as in a nightmare. He dared not peer at his watch. He wanted only to escape, but one thing remained to be done. Fumbling in a pocket of his jacket, he took out Arlene's engraved wedding ring, held it at a height of a couple of feet, then let it drop.

It landed in a shallow gully between flagstones and turf, partially obscured by stray tendrils of greenery. Once more, Pike stepped back for an assessment.

Seconds later he was back at the gate. Dragging it shut, he re-engaged the metal hoop, ensuring that it came to rest in the groove that it had already worn in the ancient mould covering the post. Collapsing into the driving seat of the van, he fingered the ignition key and hesitated.

There was no help for it. A jerk thrust life into the motor, splitting the night silence. Heart in mouth, Pike engaged reverse gear, backed up, swung the van around, set off at a low chuckle back along the track.

Six minutes later, at cruising speed on the ring road, nausea attacked him. He pulled into a lay-by and stayed there until he had recovered sufficiently to complete the journey back to the town centre.

# CHAPTER 8

'She's not back *yet*?'

The sleep-impregnated voice of Arlene's mother conveyed alarm and incredulity in equal proportions from the landing. Seconds later she appeared on the stairs, hair askew, cheeks glistening with cold cream, dressing-gown flopping at the neck. 'Where on earth can she be,' she demanded, 'all this time?'

She joined her husband and Pike in the ground-floor lobby of their maisonette. A woman of sturdy build, inches taller than either of them, she seemed to fill the limited space with an odd blend of feminine fluffiness and matriarchal dominance. She gave Pike a stare of cordial distaste. 'Do you know it's nearly two in the morning?'

This, Pike replied humbly, was the reason he had called

round. 'I thought, if she was here, I could drive her home. I don't like the idea of her being out by herself, this time of a night.'

'Well, she's not here. We'd have phoned you back if she'd turned up. When we didn't hear again, we assumed she'd come home and everything was all right.' Her survey became piercing. 'You've had a row with her, I take it?'

'No, Mrs Spelding. Nothing like that. Like I said when I rang, she just went outside a bit before ten o'clock to do some work on the van. Then she faded out on me. I've not seen her since.'

A cough came from the reedy throat of Arlene's father, a harassed-looking man with features as gaunt as his wife's were pneumatic. 'You're positive you'd, um, said nothing?'

'I'd know, wouldn't I, if I had?'

'Not necessarily,' said his father-in-law drily. 'Did she take the van, wherever she's gone?'

'No. This is the point. She went off on foot, or else maybe thumbed a lift. She left the van by the shed. I've just been out in it, looking for her. On my way back—'

'You know what I'm wondering?' Mrs Spelding interrupted, addressing her husband. 'I'm wondering if she's been fretting about Donald. You know how responsible she's always felt for him. She was saying on Friday, she didn't much care for the looks of this crowd he's got in with. Just a bunch of layabouts. This squat they're sharing . . . it's barely legal, if you ask me. Arlene thought so too. I'm wondering if she suddenly decided to call round there, on impulse, to see how Donald's getting on.'

'If she had, wouldn't she have taken the van?'

'Naturally she would,' Pike interposed. 'And she's not with her brother, Mrs Spelding. I called in there myself. Donald's not seen her for more than a fortnight.'

'Then she must have—'

'I've tried everyone. Nobody's clapped eyes on her since

ten o'clock. So I reckon we should notify the police.'

Wordlessly, Mr Spelding made for the stairs, which led to the first-floor living-room where the telephone was situated. His wife turned an accusative eye upon Pike.

'Why didn't you call them sooner?'

'Seemed silly to panic, Mrs Spelding. I kept thinking she'd arrive back any minute.'

'Has she done anything like this before?'

'Not quite like this. She comes in late from night class, quite often.'

His mother-in-law's eyebrows swept together. 'How late?'

Pike shrugged. 'Midnight. Soon after. It varies.'

'I thought they finished at nine?'

'That's right. Only she stops behind, I suppose, for a chinwag with the others. Dare say they wander out for a drink. You know how it is, with a crowd.'

'Arlene,' Mrs Spelding said icily, 'is not that kind of a girl. She wouldn't stay out drinking into the small hours. I know her too well. Haven't you spoken to her about it?'

'Me? None of my business. Arlene's a free agent, got her own life to lead.'

'That's really not good enough. You're responsible for her safety, Marvin. You can't just—'

'I appreciate that. I'm looking for her now, aren't I? It's not like a normal occasion. I mean, she'd already got back early from night class. All she did was nip outside again to do ten minutes' work on the van. That's the difference.'

'Talking of normality,' said Mrs Spelding in ponderous style, 'is there anything that strikes you about Arlene's behaviour lately? Anything out of the ordinary?'

Pike meditated deeply.

'There *could* have been something niggling at her,' he admitted. 'Not on the domestic side, don't get me wrong. No hassles there, to speak of. But once or twice she has seemed sort of . . . absent-minded, to be quite honest with you. Like as if she had her mind on something else. I put it down to this maintenance class of hers, only she says she—'

'I've phoned your house again,' Mr Spelding informed Pike from the stairs. 'Still no reply, so obviously she's not back. Then I got on to the police. They—'

'What did they say?' beseeched his wife.

'After I'd explained the circumstances, the desk sergeant got interested and took some details. If she gets back, they want us to tell them at once. Meanwhile they're alerting their patrols.' Pike's father-in-law gazed a little helplessly over the banisters. 'All they can do, isn't it? For the moment. The sergeant seemed convinced she'll turn up of her own accord, before long.'

''Course she will,' Pike declared. He patted Mrs Spelding's shoulder, which twitched under the contact. 'Arlene can look after herself, don't you worry. Apt to make you nervous, what you read nowadays, but she'll be okay, you mark my words.'

Mrs Spelding sniffed twice and turned away. 'I hope so, Marvin. Let us know, won't you, the moment she gets in?'

Home again, Pike ran a hot bath and sank himself into its welcoming depths. Every limb and muscle ached. A soil-streak had somehow ducked under his trouser-leg to decorate his shin. He sponged it off. The warm water relaxed him, fed sleep into his brain.

Forcing himself to sit upright, he recaptured his grip upon himself. Rest could come later.

As he finished towelling off, the doorbell rang downstairs. Hurriedly dragging on a clean shirt and his reserve pair of trousers, he stowed the other garments in the wash-basket and jammed the lid on before hastening down to answer the follow-up blast, which had a no-nonsense, peremptory sound to it. Pausing in the passage, he took two or three deep breaths, slowed his movements, before opening the street door.

'Mr Marvin Pike?'

'That's me. You got a message from my father-in-law?'

'The message I got,' returned the uniformed police-constable who stood in the porch, 'came from my sarge. Your wife's done a vanishing act, I'm given to understand. Any reappearance, so far?'

He wasn't as youthful as some of them were inclined to look, nowadays. A mature thirty, in Pike's judge-ment, with an air of resignation to the fact that the world was a touchy place, rife with questionable events. He was holding his peaked cap at waist level, leaving his dense, black or dark-brown hair slightly flattened. Behind him, a Panda car with its sidelights on was parked at the kerbside.

'Not a word of her,' Pike told him. 'Want to come in for a sec?'

Accepting the invitation as a matter of course, the con-stable stepped past him, biffing an elbow on the doorframe and hissing through his teeth as he touched down on the uncarpeted floor of the passage. 'Bit cramped for space,' Pike apologized, indicating the living-room door. 'Picked this place up cheap a few years back and meant to flog it pretty quick, only somehow . . .'

'These days,' observed the constable, giving the living-room a fish-eye survey as he arrived in the doorway, 'the in-word is *compact*. Mind you, that's not always the way the housewife sees it. She does tend to prefer a bit of elbow-room. Can't blame her, can you?'

Pike looked at him. 'If it's my wife you're referring to, she's not run off because—'

'No, no. Didn't mean to imply that. Likes it here, I expect. Handy for the kiddies.'

'We've no children.'

'Ah. Just the two of you? Or at this precise moment, one

of you.' The constable bent his inspection upon Arlene's armchair with its squashed cushion and its drapery of green cardigan. From there his gaze roamed on to the table and curtains. 'You're going to see this,' he predicted, 'as a fairly silly question, but it's as well to get it disposed of early on in the discussion. You *have* carried out a thorough search of *all* the rooms?'

'In my opinion,' Pike said piously, 'it's a perfectly good question. My wife could easily have slipped back into the house while I was looking for her outside, then come over faint and fallen inside the wardrobe or somewhere. I've read of dafter things. So, the answer is, I've searched at least twice in every place I can think of. No luck.'

'Slipped back from where, sir? I've not been given the details.'

Pike explained about the van. The constable gave him a whimsical look. 'Your wife takes care of the oil can and the adjustable spanner?'

Pike explained about the maintenance class. The constable looked impressed. 'Wish my good lady had similar ambitions. Save me no end of sweat, of a weekend.'

He ruminated. 'So,' he resumed presently, giving the corner of the tablecloth a twitch to level the surface. 'Your wife's not with any of her family? You've checked? And she hasn't some bosom chum she might run to, on a whim? In any case, sir, she'd have let you know. Would she not? No reason for keeping you in suspense. Not as if there'd been harsh words exchanged . . . absolutely not. All quiet and serene, till she upped and vanished. Very puzzling. Upsetting for you.'

'You can say that again.'

'This van of yours. Where's it kept?'

'I'll show you,' said Pike.

Outside, the constable seemed to take more interest in the rear alleyway than in the van itself. Equipped with a flashlamp from his car, he searched not only the immediate precincts but the full length of the access, aiming the beam into and beneath every exposed vehicle and testing the door handles. The entrance to each garden was not neglected, either. Every gate was rattled, every fence peered over. On the return trip, he asked for the van keys, opened it up and carried out a moderately thorough inspection of the interior, finishing with a closer scrutiny of the rear loading doors which he opened and shut several times in a thoughtful manner. 'Ever had any trouble with these, sir?'

'Trouble? No.'

'Never flown open as you've gone along?'

'Not when I've been driving it.'

Closing and securing the doors, the constable leaned against them and appeared to be studying the paintwork. 'You know, Mr Pike, she'll probably show up around breakfast-time, right as ninepence.'

'I'm hoping so.'

'In the meantime, though, we have to take it a bit seriously. Any bother with intruders round here lately?'

'Prowlers, you mean?' Pike shook his head. 'Generally speaking, it's a pretty quiet neighbourhood. Not a lot for anyone to lift, in a street like this.'

'I wouldn't bank on it, sir. Some of these tearaways . . . Smash a back window and hop inside, soon as blink.'

'What's this to do with my wife?'

The constable looked wounded. 'When a young woman melts into the night, as you might say, we have to take a look at all sides of the equation. Assuming that no—hum —exterior agency was involved, then of course we're left with the personal factor.'

'Personal?'

'To put it bluntly, sir, your wife's state of mind when she came out here last evening. Like it or not, we have to consider that this could lie at the root of the problem.'

'You're suggesting,' said Pike after an interval, 'that my wife was mentally disturbed in some way?'

'Not was, sir. Is. Mustn't write her off just yet, must we?'

When he came to the door, Alec Jones was still in shirtsleeves and looked as though he had slept in his denims. He blinked blearily at Pike. 'Hi, fellah. Arlene get back yet?'

'Still no word. Mind if I come in?'

With an apprehensive glance across a shoulder, Jones stepped aside. 'Pat's at the toast-and-marmalade stage,' he said with an assumption of joviality. 'No, no, it's okay—she won't mind. Might offer you coffee. You look like you could do with some. Pat! Marvin's here.'

'Send him through.'

Jones's pear-shaped wife was munching while standing up, pouring orange juice from a carton into a tumbler. Ill-advisedly, she too was wearing jeans, overhung by a sweater three sizes below requirements; the total effect was that of an airship inflated by helium. At Pike's entrance she turned. Embedded in a pudding face, her eyes were small and watchful, the tools of the school sneak. She was not a local. With Jones, she had arrived in the area four years previously from the North; and yet Pike had always nursed the uneasy feeling that in childhood they had been closely associated, he and she, and that either could divine at any given moment what the other was thinking. This morning she seemed almost to welcome his appearance.

'Hi, Marvin. No news yet, then?'

Pike spread his arms. 'Had the law pay us a visit, earlier. They reckon they're looking into it.'

'What time did they call?'

'Around three, it must have been. Just a bloke in a Panda. Didn't do much.'

'Not a lot he could do, I suppose. Not unless . . .' The pinprick eyes met those of her husband, rested there briefly before turning back to Pike. 'Take a seat for a minute. You look really bushed.'

Pike committed himself to the concavity of a leather-seated upright chair of hideous design, while she placed an immense elbow against some nearby wall-shelving stocked with video-tapes and took one or two bubbling inhalations of the orange juice, looking down at him like a sow keeping a watchful eye on its litter. 'I was just saying to Alec, it's bad enough having a business to run these days, never mind domestic hassle on top. I mean, you need your sleep, don't you?' She made it sound like a spoonful of something that Pike ought to be taking twice a day after meals. 'Don't suppose you managed to snatch a wink last night. I know I wouldn't have.'

'I was waiting for the phone to ring.'

'And of course it never does. Not when you're hoping it might.' More orange juice gurgled down. 'This copper, did he say what they were going to do?'

'Not in so many words. Up to his chief, I dare say.'

'Not a bad sort, was he?'

Pike glanced up sharply. 'Did you see him?'

She nodded complacently. 'Not at three o'clock, though. He called here, just an hour or so ago. Said he'd been talking to you.'

'What else did he say?'

'He needed some Assistance,' she said importantly. 'Wanted to know if we'd heard anything in the night. And he was asking about Arlene.'

'Asking what about her?'

'Don't panic, Marvin. Just ordinary things. Whether or not she'd a regular routine, whether she was inclined to do things on impulse . . . All that.'

'Shouldn't think there was much you could tell him. Was there?'

'We did our best,' volunteered Jones, hovering at the breakfast-table.

Draining the tumbler, Pat set it down amid the videotapes and wiped her mouth daintily with a tissue. 'Don't get us wrong, Marvin. It's not as if I'm fond of gossip . . .'

'Gossip? How d'you mean, gossip?'

'I'm not meaning to imply there's *been* gossip. Not as such. It's only what Arlene mentioned to me herself. In confidence, I may say. Only when it's a copper that's asking . . .'

'What was he asking about, Pat?'

'Nothing. In particular. Just anything we might know, either of us, about the . . . situation. As I told him, we've never been ones to pry into people's—'

'What flaming situation? What did you tell him?'

'I told him,' Pat said with dignified restraint, 'exactly what Arlene herself told me. Not that it's relevant, probably. That's for him to decide. A month or two back it was. She was in here for a cup of tea and a natter—I thought she needed cheering up—and she was saying how things seemed to get on top of her, so I said, Why was that? And she said, Oh, she hated deceit but there were times when you couldn't seem to get away from it, and what would I do in her place? So I said, What place might that be? and she said . . .'

Pat paused for lung-replenishment. 'Sorry, Marvin. Unless you know about this already, it'll come as a bit of a shock.'

'Tell us, anyway.'

'She said,' Pat repeated, lingering over the syllables, 'that people sometimes got Involved with other people practically before they knew it was happening . . . and she went on to mention this bloke. She gave me to understand she was Seeing Him.'

Pike stared at the toast-rack. 'I see.'

'Sorry, pet, but you did ask.'

'Did she mention a name?'

'Never let on about that. Actually, she didn't say much at

all, really. Just referred to this . . . friendship and made me promise to keep quiet about it, which I did, of course. Even to Alec. I wouldn't have said anything now, only seeing that Constable Evans was making these inquiries . . .'

'I understand. You probably did right, Pat. I'm glad you've told me. It could explain a lot of things.' Pike continued to gaze bleakly at the tableware. 'I'd no idea. Bit blind, I expect. Did think she'd been broody for the past few months, but I put it down to . . . y'know. Female moods. I never imagined . . .'

'Well, you wouldn't, would you?' Pat regarded him with a certain self-satisfied compassion. 'A woman sees these things more. I'd had my suspicions, I must say. The way she was behaving. This is what made me wonder . . .'

'Made you wonder?' prompted Pike, looking up at her entreatingly.

'Whether she might be getting really serious about it. Planning something.'

'How d'you mean?' Pike injected a note of terror into his voice.

'Not for me to say, is it? I'm just guessing. Anyhow, this is what I told Constable Evans just now, and he seemed to think it might be important. Said he'd probably be having a word with you about it. Coffee, pet? Pour Marvin a cup, love. Black, with lots of sugar. Very soothing for the nerves, when you've had bad news.'

## CHAPTER 9

For no obvious reason, trade at Margar that morning was brisker than usual. Pike welcomed the activity for more reasons than one: it kept his mind off things.

'Why,' he demanded of Gail as she emerged from the

stockroom with fresh supplies of stationery, 'can't it always be like this? We might get somewhere.'

'Another morning, we hang about twiddling our thumbs.' Gail sounded preoccupied. 'Makes no sense.'

'If it's sense you're looking for,' Pike returned philosophically, 'you don't come into retail. They the last of the pads?'

'Nearly.' Depositing the boxful, she began stocking the glass shelves behind the counter, her floppy attire billowing to her movements. 'There's a load of other stuff we need, too. Fibre-tip pens. Sticky tape . . .'

'I'll be talking to Gareth later.'

Intent on her task, Gail fell silent. A lull had followed the frenzy of custom: for almost the first time that day, they had the shop to themselves and Pike had unwanted space in which to think. Tension was mounting in his chest and stomach. How long, he wondered, before a development occurred? It could be weeks. Months, even. Years? Anything was possible. If Arlene were to remain on the missing persons file, and no connection were traced back to Gareth . . .

But it had to be. Pike, he congratulated himself, had laid the trail with some adroitness. Any investigating force worth its salt must sooner or later find itself steered inexorably in the direction of his partner; no other avenue could suggest itself. The testimony of Pat and Alec Jones, by itself, ought to be sufficient.

Pike had few illusions. According to Pat, no name had been mentioned by Arlene, but quite simply Pike didn't believe her. She knew who it was, all right. And, in her helpful way, she would undoubtedly have passed the information to Constable Evans, who in turn could be relied upon to relay it to his superiors or else pursue his own inquiries. Gareth, in short, could expect an interrogation in the near future, one that he might not relish.

But how persistent, at this stage, would the police turn out to be?

Worrying about it, Pike caught the movement of a figure across the pavement outside. With a lurch of the heart, he also spotted the Panda car parked at the kerb. Although he had been prepared for another visitation from Constable Evans, the actuality still came as a jolt. He did his best to react normally.

'Looks like we've a visit from the law.'

Gail glanced round. 'P'raps he's after a new notepad. Whoops!' The pile she was holding had shot out of her grasp to distribute themselves over the shop floor. 'Now look what you made us do.' She crawled in pursuit of the merchandise. Pike contrived a chortle.

'Guilty conscience, obviously. Must be those sweaty palms.'

A fine position he was in, to joke of sweat. His own skin was exuding the stuff by the pint. And his abrupt realization that it was not Constable Evans but an altogether weightier, more deliberate-moving sample of officialdom who was now placing his bulk against the swing door and easing himself through, did nothing to dry him out. He waited at the counter. Outwardly he was calm, or hoped he was. His cheeks, unfortunately, were starting to burn. He knew the symptoms. A glance at his reflection would have shown him two bright crimson spots, one on each side of the nose, twin craters betraying the volcano. How astute was this sergeant? At first sight, he had a friendly air. Only he wasn't smiling.

'Mr Pike? They said I might find you here. Got a few moments, sir?'

'First I've had all morning, to tell you the honest truth.' Steaming the creases out of his voice, Pike replaced it with the monotone of subdued anxiety and brought his eyebrows together in a demonstration of eagerness. 'Not heard from my wife, have you? I've been waiting to—'

'Somewhere private we can talk?' The sergeant glanced around, catching sight of Gail still crawling about the floor, retrieving pads. 'You've got help, I see.'

Gail's flushed face showed itself above the counter. 'Not much help at the moment,' she mumbled. She held out a pad. 'Fancy one? Compliments of the house.'

'Thank you.' He took it gravely. Slightly taken aback, she threw Pike a dubious look and shrugged a semi-apology. Pike grinned heroically.

'Always a hefty discount for the constabulary.' He indicated the stockroom door. 'You'd better go through, Sarge. Manage on your own, Gail, for a little while?'

'Long as nobody comes in, wanting to know about VAT returns.' The girl was eyeing him curiously. Ignoring her unspoken question, he pursued the sergeant into the small, airless room at the back of the shop, closed the door behind them and switched on another light, illuminating the pockets of filth that had been allowed to accumulate between stacked cartons on the shelves and floor. He propped himself against a wall-rack.

'I've not told my assistant,' he explained, 'about my wife going missing. That is what you've come about?'

The sergeant's facial expression was, in an odd way, blank and yet purposeful. 'You've heard nothing from her yourself as yet, Mr Pike, I'm right in assuming?'

Pike shook a worried head. 'Not a whisper. I did wonder if she might be home by now, but when I rang twenty minutes ago there was still no reply.' He had made a point of calling at half-hourly intervals since his arrival in the shop at eight-fifteen. 'Mind you, if she's out to teach me a lesson or something, she could be just letting it ring.'

'Any special reason, sir, she might be wanting to teach you a lesson?'

Pike put on his helpless look. 'To be quite honest with you, Sarge, I've been bashing my brains to put my finger on something, but it beats me. I've not been late for any meals lately, as I can recall. She's not asked for cash that I couldn't let her have. Everything's been great. That is . . .'

He hesitated. The sergeant assessed him. 'You were about to say something else?'

'Only that I had some slightly unsettling information passed on to me this morning, by a neighbour. Concerning my wife. A personal matter.'

The sergeant waited. Pike went on, 'It might or might not explain her absence, but if you don't mind I'd rather not say any more, just at the moment. Looking back, what I can say is that she certainly hasn't been one hundred per cent herself in the past few weeks. I do realize that now. In fact, not long ago she seemed so restless that I suggested we went away somewhere for a holiday, but she said she could do without. So I didn't push it.'

'Would that have been practicable?'

'Going away, you mean? It would have meant staff problems,' Pike admitted. 'I'd have needed to get someone in. The girl's a trier, but she could never have managed on her own.'

'Hard to get reliable people, is it?'

'Next to impossible.'

'Couldn't your partner have held the fort for a week or two?'

'How did you know I had a partner?'

The sergeant looked evasive. 'Your next-door neighbours happened to mention it to our PC Evans.'

'Did they now? Funny, the amount of interest that's worked up when somebody goes missing. On the other hand,' Pike added generously, 'I appreciate they'd have wanted to let the constable know of anything that might help him to make inquiries. Have to ask around, don't you, in these cases? I can see that.'

The sergeant came as near to looking ill at ease as his natural self-possession permitted. 'This unsettling information you were talking about just now. It wouldn't have had anything to do with your partner?'

'It might.'

'With regard to the business?'

'Not the business, no.'

'A personal matter, I think you said.' The sergeant paused once more. Pike looked back at him in silence. 'Relating to Mr Somers,' the sergeant persevered, 'and also your wife. Are we getting anywhere near the nub of the matter?'

'Look, Sarge,' Pike said on a note of candour, 'we might as well stop beating about the bush. Obviously Mrs Jones told the constable more or less what she told me this morning, which is that my wife and my partner have been . . . seeing one another. Right?'

'If they had,' the sergeant said cautiously, 'would that bother you a lot? If you don't mind me saying so, you sound fairly relaxed about it.'

'I've reason to be. There's nothing in it, that's why. I know my wife and she's just not the type. If she was playing around—with anybody—I'd know soon enough. As for Gareth, that's ridiculous. We've all known each other since we were at school. Besides . . .'

'Besides what, Mr Pike?'

'I phoned Gareth last night, after my wife vanished, and he was quite definite she wasn't with him.'

'And you believed him?'

'Of course I believed him. We've never—'

Pike stopped and looked away, frowning. The sergeant didn't interrupt. After several moments of scowling into vacancy, Pike returned to him with a start. 'I still reckon you're barking up the wrong tree. If Arlene and Gareth had been doing anything behind my back, I'm damn sure I'd have got wind of it. You've got me a bit worried now, though, I have to admit. Should I pop over to his place, in your opinion? Find out for sure?'

'I wouldn't do that, sir.'

'Why not? It's the only way to check.'

'Leave it to us, sir, that's my advice. We'll notify you of any developments.'

Pike stared. 'You seem to be taking a lot of interest. I mean, it's just a domestic issue, surely? I've not had much experience, but I'd have thought that if you're taking the view that my wife's simply walked out on me for someone else . . .'

Hoisting his bulk from the middle shelf on to which it had subsided, the sergeant looking down at him from an Olympian altitude and, like Zeus about to hurl a bolt, rumblingly cleared his throat.

'The reason we're taking such an interest, Mr Pike, is that it's more than a mere domestic issue, I'm greatly afraid. Can you stomach a dose of bad news?'

The frown returned involuntarily to Pike's face. Without warning, his heart performed an apparently spontaneous rat-tat-tat against his chest-lining, causing him to lose breath. 'What is it?' he asked faintly.

'It's about your partner, Mr Somers. He's been found stabbed to death at his home.'


At the window end of the counter, Gail was selling tubes of peppermints to a trio of small girls in school uniform, including straw boaters. Navigating blindly between them, Pike was dimly aware that he had knocked off the headgear of one of them with an elbow. He muttered an apology.

'Sarge wants a word with you,' he said hoarsely to Gail. 'I'll take over here.'

Her mouth fell open. 'See me? What about?'

'You'll find out.' As she rounded the end of the counter to pass him, Pike arrested her progress by gripping her arm.

He lowered his voice. 'Gail, listen a minute. Don't tell him what I was saying.'

'Huh?' She wrinkled her nose, struggling to comprehend.

'About Gareth. What we were talking about yesterday. Not a word, understand? We never had that conversation.'

Okay,' she said in a tone of perplexity. 'If you say so.' Pausing to retrieve the unseated straw hat, she handed it back to its owner before hurrying off to the stockroom door, where she hesitated, looked back doubtfully at Pike, elevated a thumb, turned the door handle and went inside. The door shut again. Pike was left holding half a dozen bargain packs of peppermint cylinders at which he stared blankly, wondering how they had got into his hand.

A timid voice said, 'They're ours, mister.'

He shook his head, clearing it momentarily. 'Not till you've paid for 'em, they're not.'

'We was just going to.'

'Let's see your money, then.'

Tenpenny pieces came at him. He dropped several, heard them roll across the floor. The girls dived in pursuit. Passively awaiting their return, he accepted the money a second time, stared hard at the change figure recorded in green on the till, tried to recall how to assemble the required amount. In the end he scooped up a handful of coins, poured a few of each into small recipient palms and watched the silent retreat of the trio from the shop, unable to calculate whether he had overpaid or defrauded them, and caring neither way. The instant they were gone, he strode to the door and locked it, turned the CLOSED sign to face the street, pulled down the blind. Returning to the till, he closed it and switched off. After this he approached the stockroom door, rapped twice, opened it and inserted his head.

'I'm shutting for the day,' he announced.

The sergeant, who was in a huddle with Gail, pivoted to

eye him. 'Good thinking, I'd say. We'll be needing to see you again, Mr Pike, a little later on.'

'I'm available now.'

'First, I've a few more questions to put to Miss Franklin here.' The sergeant glanced significantly at the gap in the doorway.

'What do you want me to do, in the meantime?'

'Just stick around.'

Pike retired once more into the shop. Pacing restlessly, he adjusted the positions of a few items in showcases, heaved a toy rack two feet further to the left to make more space available in front of the counter—an improvement that his subconscious had been urging him to make for months. Slowly, with much creaking and grinding, his brain was starting to function again. Coming to rest by the window display, he stood gazing out at the parade.

Parked cars. Meters. The bright green litter bin fastened to a lamp-post. Ten yards further along, the telephone call-box outside the sub-Post Office. Like a stencil, the scene stamped itself clearly and yet two-dimensionally upon the surface of his mind, informative without being meaningful. As he stood there, two elderly women tottered up to the shop door, which shook to the weight of the more robust of the pair. From the shelter of the blind, Pike could see her standing outraged in the centre of the pavement, peering, for some reason, at the upper windows while exchanging words with her more decrepit companion. Both of them came nearer to inspect intensively the CLOSED placard. One of them pointed, and they shuffled off towards the sub-Post-Office and the Patels.

Somers, thought Pike, would not have approved.

He was still finding it hard to come to terms with the news he had just received. Working out the implications was impossible. Intellectually, he knew that his erstwhile partner was no longer a feature of the landscape; despite all that he could do, however, his imagination, for all its limitations, insisted upon sketching him in. Presently, with a physical shake of the body like a dog's as it emerged from water, he returned to the till and embarked on the process of emptying the drawers, transferring the morning's takings —considerable for once—into canvas bags for depositing at the bank. The routine provided a much-needed breathing space. By the time Gail reappeared with the sergeant in tow, Pike was motoring again, alert to route obstacles.

'Got all you want, for the moment?'

'I'd like you to come along to the station, Mr Pike, this afternoon at your convenience.' The sergeant's polite turn of phrase was somehow no solace. 'Ask for the Chief Inspector, will you? Forester's the name. Bloke in charge of the case.'

'What time's best?'

'Two-thirty, three.' The sergeant gestured vaguely. 'He'll be there. Thanks for your help, both of you. Sorry to have to be the one to hit you with it.'

Tossing the canvas bags into a leather pouch, Pike snapped the fasteners. 'I've not heard yet how . . . what happened, exactly. Was it . . . y'know, violent?'

'Chief'll fill you in,' the sergeant replied crisply. 'I'll be away, then. How do I get out of here? Oh, I'm with you. Not terribly smart, this brand of catch. Easily forced. Have a word with Chubbs, my advice. Could pay you. Thanks once again.'

The door slammed back. Outside, the Panda car was started up, driven off. Resetting the lock, Pike turned, wandered back to the counter. Gail sat on the end of it. Their eyes met.

He gave a slight shake of the head. 'Bit of a zonker, that.'

'Shattering.' Exploratively she put out a hand, rested it upon the glass surface between them. Unthinkingly, Pike covered it with one of his own, applied pressure.

'Took the wind out of us,' he muttered. 'Wasn't expecting it.'

Gail inspected their interlocked fingers. 'Rotten bit of news,' she ventured after a moment. 'Gareth, of all people.'

'What was he asking you?'

Her face jerked up. 'Who? Oh—you mean the sergeant? Nothing much, really. Just when I last saw Gareth, like. What sort of mood he was in. Stuff like that.' On a note of reassurance she added, 'Not as I could tell him a lot. Hardly anythink, in fact.'

'That's my girl,' Pike said absently. He gave her fingers a squeeze.

Breaking another silence, she said, 'Why didn't you want me to . . . ?'

'Obvious, isn't it? Don't want 'em jumping to conclusions, do I?'

'The police? Reckon they would?'

'No sense in giving 'em half a chance. I mean, I'm not exactly in a good position here, Gail. My wife's gone missing and my partner's been . . . Smells a bit, doesn't it? You have to admit that.'

Gail pondered.

'If they knew,' she observed finally, 'that *you* knew she'd been seeing him . . . On top of the stock fiddle, it could make them start wondering, couldn't it? You might be right. I see now, Marvin, why you didn't want us to say nothing.'

'Thanks for cottoning on.'

She blinked. 'I didn't, not straight away. But I could see you was anxious, so I kept me lips buttoned when the sergeant got too nosey. Then when he said what had happened . . . Never had such a shock in me life.'

Releasing her hand, Pike picked up the pouch. 'Seeing as we're shut,' he suggested, 'how about some lunch? I mean a brandy or something, at the Royal Oak? I don't think I want to eat.'

'Me neither. A drink might set us up. Let's go.'

At the door he halted. 'You say the sergeant told you what happened. He didn't say much to me. Just that Gareth was stabbed. What was it, a knife or something?'

Gail slipped the door-catch. 'Not a knife,' she said. 'A pair of scissors.' She nodded towards a display rack standing in a corner of the shop. 'Same type as that lot over there. I've not flogged any yet, have you? There's a pair missing, though. I noticed they'd gone, yesterday.'


# CHAPTER 10

The brandy seemed to help. A lifelong beer-drinker, Pike had never subscribed to the notion that more spirituous compounds might achieve speedier results; but circumstances altered cases. In this instance, he had to allow that after half an hour things started to matter less. Or appear to do so. After forty minutes, the future stopped being menacing and became merely indefinite. He was able to confront it again, squarely. He had an urgent need to talk.

'About those scissors . . .' he began.

Gail intervened. 'I could be wrong, you know. P'raps we was a pair short at the start. Don't remember noticing, do you, when we hung 'em on the rack?'

Pike agreed that he had taken no account of numbers or deficiencies. 'That sarge—he definitely said it was a pair just like 'em that was used for . . . ?'

'So he reckoned.'

'Bit small, aren't they?'

'Well, you wouldn't need anything too . . .' Gail gulped. Pausing to fortify herself with a mouthful of cognac, she resumed: 'I've been thinking. That display we've got at the shop—it's in reach of anybody, right? Anyone could've lifted a pair. Might have been Gareth, come to that. He could've taken them home himself.'

Pike nodded solemnly. 'So he could. And knowing what we do about him, he probably did. Police have got 'em now, I suppose?'

'Oh no. They've not found them.'

Pike stared. 'Well, in that case, how do they know—'

'They can tell,' she explained, 'from their examinations, like, the kind of weapon that was used.' She drank again. 'It was scissors, all right. Only they're still missing.'

'No chance it was suicide, then.'

'Can't see Gareth wanting to kill himself, can you? He was having too good a time. Unless . . .'

'Unless what?'

'He was afraid of what else you might find out. About Arlene, I mean, as well as the accounts and that.'

Pike was silent. He was starting to regret having mentioned anything of these matters to Gail, although there was nothing to be done about it now. He couldn't recall the words. Perhaps misinterpreting his sudden reticence, she pursued the topic with ingenuous avidity.

'It's a thought, isn't it? P'raps he was more worried than he let on. For all you know, he could've been conning you out of thousands . . .'

'He was,' Pike couldn't help interjecting.

'There you are, then!' Gail puffed her cheeks. 'If he knew you was on to him . . . Never surprise me if he panicked, like. Wasn't up to facing the music, so . . . What do you think?'

Pike frowned. 'The cops,' he objected, 'generally have a fair idea if it's suicide or not. From the way he spoke, I don't reckon that sarge was thinking down those lines.'

Discouraged, Gail paused for reflection, swivelling her knees to enable an elderly couple to squeeze past them on their way to the next alcove. When they were out of earshot she said, 'Here, look. Somethink else I've thought of. What about Arlene?'

'What about her?'

'She could just as easily have lifted them scissors. She come into the shop, didn't she, one day last week? Thursday. She only stayed twenty minutes, but she'd have had loads of time to help herself, if she wanted.'

Pike lowered his brandy glass to stare at her. 'What's that supposed to mean?'

'She's gone missing, right? Since last night. We know she's been seeing Gareth. What if they had a bust-up? She could've . . . Well.' Gail took a quick breath. 'Used the scissors on him, then made a run for it.'

Pike choked a little. 'That's the craziest thing I ever heard. Why would she want to do a thing like that?'

'She might not have *planned* to,' Gail pointed out earnestly. 'What if she just went to see him, same as she always did, and they had this sudden quarrel? If she'd the scissors with her—in her bag, say—what was to stop her? Wouldn't take a lot of muscle, as long as she took him by surprise.'

Taking an edgy sip of the remaining brandy, Pike swirled it around his mouth and swallowed with a shudder. 'I wouldn't mention anything like that to the law. Let 'em work it out for themselves.'

'All right, Marve, if you'd sooner I didn't. Just struck me as funny, that's all—Gareth copping it, and Arlene fading out at the same time. Don't you reckon? But I'll keep it to meself, if that's what you want.'

'This chief inspector bloke—if he's got any brains he'll put two and two together, anyway.'

'I expect he will.' Gail regarded him sidelong: a look of appraisal. 'Still fond of Arlene, aren't you, Marvin? Have her back, if she turns up?'

He said gruffly, 'What do you think?'

*

Chief Inspector Forester of the CID was not as Pike had pictured him. A tall, lean individual with a beaked nose above a firm mouth pencilled in by a wisp of a moustache; well-cut suit with striped necktie; a personal manner of effortless authority, ballasted by surroundings of a traditional, oak-panelled nature . . . this was the image that Pike had conjured from nothing. The reality was not only different, but a severe let-down. He was ill-prepared, he discovered, for the thickset, imperfectly shaven gingerhead of less than average stature who was now scanning him unemotionally from the opposite side of a metal desk strewn with what looked like crumpled discards from an abandoned filing system. Nor did Pike appreciate having to reiterate what he had already recounted, in detail, to both Police Constable Evans and the sergeant. Finally, he resented being pressed for corroboration that it was impossible to supply. His own tone, he noticed, was taking on a progressively greater degree of petulance.

'I just motored around, looking for her. No law against that, is there?'

'What area did you cover?' Chief Inspector Forester's enunciation suggested Tyneside origins, although Pike classified it less precisely: to him, this pushy copper with a gash where his mouth belonged was simply a person who hailed from that dark region known to South Midlanders as The North, a factor which was not conducive to rapport.

'To be quite honest with you, Chief, I wasn't taking that much notice. Too concerned about my wife. All I did was drive up and down streets, watching out for her.'

'How long for?'

'Hour and a half . . . two hours. I don't honestly remember. I do know I got home a little after two.'

'So you went out soon after midnight?'

Pike lifted irritable shoulders. 'Might have been. I never checked.'

'Too preoccupied about your wife.' Forester said it on a musing note that seemed to imply more than its face value, pausing marginally before his selection of the second word. As he spoke, he was consulting what appeared to be a torn-off section of a computer print-out. Removing his gaze from it eventually, he squinted at Pike across the metallic surface of the desk.

'Aside from your wife's parents, did you call in on any other of her relatives in the course of this grand tour of the district?'

'As I told the other officers,' Pike said with measured patience, 'I'd already rung some of them from home. I didn't fancy the idea of knocking them up afterwards.'

'But you did try her mum and dad.'

'Only as a last resort.'

'*A last resort?*' Forester echoed the phrase in accented wonderment. 'First port of call, I'd have imagined. When a wife flounces out, she's fairly liable to scuttle home to mother, in my book.'

'She didn't flounce. I told you. I told the others. She went outside to see to the van, that's all. There wasn't any disagreement.'

'The van . . .'

Forester perused the print-out again, humming unmelodiously to himself. He glanced up. 'Had it long, have you?'

'Three or four years. But it's older than that.'

'Happy with it?'

'Not hysterically.' What was this in aid of? 'Wouldn't say no to something a bit less basic, to be quite honest with you.'

'Got anything in mind?'

Pike smiled thinly. 'No shortage of ideas. It's a question of what's feasible.'

'Not a vast amount of profit in stationery and newspapers?'

'Depends what you call profit.'

Releasing the print-out to flutter to the desk, Forester leaned back. 'My definition,' he murmured, 'would be excess of income over expenditure, sizeable enough to notice. But then, you know your own business best, I've no doubt. Come here in the van, did you?'

Pike looked him in the eye. 'It's parked outside.'

'Not on the yellow band, I trust,' the chief inspector said jocularly. 'Mind if we take a squint at it?'

'What for?'

'What for?' Forester weighed the query. 'Let's just say, you never know what you might find.'

'Your PC Evans went through it last night.'

'In darkness, at a gallop. A more leisurely inspection in the light of day could reveal something he missed.'

'Like what?'

'I don't know, do I?' the chief inspector asked reasonably. 'Not unless we find it. But it strikes me that this runabout of yours constitutes the one link we have with your wife's disappearance. After all, she was supposedly working on it at the time.'

Pike threw the keys resoundingly on to the desk. 'Take a look, then, if you want. I thought it was my partner's death you were inquiring about.'

'It is,' Forester said cryptically.

He spoke into the intercom, then took a turn about the room. Within seconds, a younger man in plain clothes presented himself. Tossing him the keys, the chief inspector stabbed a thumb at the window. 'Ford Escort van, mustard-orange, parked in the street. Take it round to the yard, Joe, and give it the eye. We have the owner's consent.'

Joe smiled charmingly at Pike. 'What am I looking for?'

His superior sighed. 'Whatever hits you as out of the ordinary. You know the drill.'

Joe withdrew, whistling. The chief inspector returned to

his chair, sat heavily, stared down at the desktop for a moment or two and then looked across.

'What were we saying? Oh yes: the demise of your former partner, Mr Gareth Summers. Somers, I beg pardon. But you pronounce it as in *comers*? Never too clear, when you only see it in print. You called him Gareth, I expect. First-name terms, were you? Good buddies?'

'We rubbed along,' Pike said tersely.

'So this must have come as quite a shock. Any reason for the killing, that occurs to you?'

'Maybe it was an accident.'

'That's a possibility, of course.' Forester gave the impression of contorting himself into crippling postures in a bid to be fair. 'Although the nature of the incident . . . Hard to be dogmatic. Something premeditated about it, to my mind. What do *you* think?'

'I might know better what to think,' Pike retorted with some astringency, 'if I'd been told more about it. All I know is that Gareth was stabbed.'

Forester nodded encouragingly. 'Mr Somers did indeed die of stab wounds. Can't fault you there.'

'You trying to set a trap for me or something?'

'A trap?'

'If not, why don't you just say what happened and leave me to deny it? Why all this pussyfooting around?'

'Deny what, Mr Pike? You're not accused of anything.'

'You could have fooled me. All these hints about how me and my partner got on . . .'

'Hints? Traps?' Forester looked pained. 'Dropping hints is no part of my job, as it happens. Inquiries are. A friend and colleague of yours has been killed, Mr Pike—snuffed out. Don't you *want* us to trace the culprit?'

'You won't track him down by asking me questions like this. You want to look into Gareth's private life. Find out who'd a motive and suchlike.'

'I do? Well, bless me. Never thought of that.' The chief inspector's irony formed a light mist over the desk. 'Since we've got on to the question of private lives, suppose we get back to your wife? Sergeant Becket, I understand, has already spoken to you about her—what shall I say?—her association with Mr Somers.'

'He did mention it.'

'What's your reaction?'

'It's a load of bull. If there'd been any hanky-panky, I'd have known about it.'

'You're positive?'

'Arlene wasn't that sort of a girl.'

'They never are. Don't you mean isn't?'

'Pardon?'

'Lest you should continue to infer,' Forester said ponderously, 'that I'm doing my best to ensnare you in some way, let me stress that I merely want it straight for the record. You referred to your wife in the past tense. I wonder why, that's all.'

'She walked out of my life, for the minute. Until she comes back, Chief, I reckon she rates as past tense, sure enough.'

The reply, Pike felt, had shown resource. He took some pride in it, especially as it had been produced against competition from internal tremors which for a hair-raising moment had threatened to rob him of speech just when he most needed it. Whether or not the chief inspector was satisfied, he couldn't determine. There was little that was assessable about his inquisitor; about any aspect, indeed, of the investigation that clearly was now in spate, pursuing a course at once traceable and yet semi-concealed in procedural thickets. He was not, Pike had to concede, being rushed. On the contrary, he was being allowed time in plenty to formulate his answers. This, paradoxically, was setting its own problems. In the space available, he was finding it difficult to decide which propositions to confirm and which to refute. He was hideously unsure of his ground.

Forester seemed to have drifted into reverie. Pike cleared his throat.

'You want the record straight, you say. Me too. I'd like to know just how my partner was found. Who by? How long was it before—'

The reopening of the door interrupted him. Back came Joe, Sphinx-faced now, holding reverently in the palm of a hand something nestling in Polythene. Emerging from trance, Forester reached out to accept the offering and brought it close to his eyes, handling it as though it had been a living virus from a germ warfare research laboratory. His nose gave a twitch.

'Under the drive-seat carpeting,' supplied Joe. 'Hard up against the seat-runner.'

'What took you so long, finding it?'

Joe simpered. 'Just happened to start there.'

Deliberately, Forester brought his hand round to where it could be seen by Pike. 'You heard, young man, what the officer said. This was found under the floor-covering at the front of your van. Care to tell us what it was doing there?'

The object was a medium-sized pair of scissors, its end-curved blades encrusted with a reddish-brown deposit.


CHAPTER 11

'Give you a hard time yesterday, did they?'

'You could say that.'

'The way you sounded,' said Gail, 'on the phone . . .'

'Sooner not talk about it. Any coffee going?'

She examined him with elder-sisterly suspicion. 'You had some breakfast?'

'Couldn't face any. Anyhow I was late getting up.'

'You should eat, you know. Did you have anything last night? What time did you get home?'

'After midnight.' Slicing the twine holding together a bundle of dailies, Pike commenced mechanically to lay them out, headlines uppermost. 'Then he'd have kept it up, the Chief, only he was practically out on his feet himself. Wants to see us again, though, later on this morning. More questions.'

'What's he trying to do—grind you down? Here, look. Anything you fancy?' Gail was scanning the confectionery shelves. 'A slab of milk chocolate might keep you going. Or I could fetch somethink in from the takeaway.'

'Don't bother, thanks.' Pike looked dully around at the shop's familiar yet suddenly claustrophobic interior. 'What I could use is some shut-eye. Never slept a wink. Just lay there, going over it all in my head. Nearly drove me potty.'

Gail went silently off to plug in the kettle in the stockroom. While she was gone, he dealt with a few early customers, among them a regular, Mrs Ball, who peered at him from beneath crocheted eyebrows while returning change to her purse. 'I heard the awful news about Mr Somers on the local radio this morning. How dreadful. You must be absolutely shattered.'

Pike said, 'It was in the evening papers yesterday.'

'Was it? I didn't buy one. Who was it—an intruder?'

'They're still trying to find out.'

'The violence these days . . .' Mrs Ball made chirruping noises. 'Somebody will just *have* to do something. You read so much about crime, but until a thing like this happens virtually on your own doorstep . . .'

Finally, in answer to Pike's prayers, Mrs Ball left the shop, still declaiming about law and order. Before a new wave could dash itself against his mental and spiritual fatigue, Pike hurried to the door, shot the lock and hung up the CLOSED sign. Then he joined Gail in the stockroom. She greeted him with some surprise.

'I've closed up again,' he explained, sinking wearily on to a box of merchandise and resting his back against the wall. 'Hopeless, trying to cope.'

'I can be looking after things . . .'

'Leave it, Gail. To hell with turnover. I've too much else on my mind, right now.'

Handing him a cup of steaming liquid, she installed herself on a low shelf opposite him and took a frowning sip or two from her share of the brew. She seemed about to say something, but didn't. Putting his head back, Pike shut his eyes. 'I suppose,' he said numbly, 'people are bound to twitter about it. Not every day of the week they've a local homicide to sink their teeth into.'

'That what the police call it?'

'They've not called it anything yet. Not to me.' Pike reopened his eyes to stare at a box of ballpens above Gail's head. 'They tie you up, you know. You think you've got an answer: then they shoot something else at you and leave you in knots. Up to all the tricks, they are.'

'Hounding you. That's what they're doing.'

'Mind you, it does look bad. Those flaming scissors. If I just knew how they could have got there . . .'

'Probably dropped out of a box you was carrying,' Gail suggested. 'Could happen, easy enough.'

''I don't remember taking anything in the van. Not recently. Anyway, how could it get under the carpet? And how about the bloodstains?'

'Could have been on the blades when they left the factory. Some worker might've cut himself.'

Pike barely heard her. 'If the grouping's the same as Gareth's . . .' He brooded. 'They'll have the result this morning, the Chief reckons. What if it matches up?'

'Wouldn't prove anything. Loads of people have the same blood group. Common knowledge.'

'Maybe, but it's not just the scissors. They've had neighbours telling 'em about the van.'

Gail paused in mid-sip. 'What about the van?'

'How they've noticed it calling at Gareth's place, of an evening. Parked outside till all hours. One busybody's spotted Arlene too, a few times. Or somebody like her.'

'So what?'

'So the Chief reckons I must have known what was going on. Doesn't see how Arlene could have taken the van there that many times without me noticing.'

Gail looked troubled. 'Well . . . You did know, didn't you?'

'I've told you,' Pike said with a touch of impatience. 'That doesn't make me a stab-happy maniac. If I'd gone over there to stick a pair of scissors into Gareth, would I have left 'em on the van floor afterwards—with bloodstains on 'em? And then used the van to drive myself to the flaming police station? Would I?'

''Course not, it's stupid.' Gail snorted loyally, threw coffee over her blouse, brushed herself down with an abstracted air. 'Did you mention to him about Arlene?'

'Mention?'

'How she could've swiped them scissors off the rack herself?'

Half-angrily, Pike shook his head. 'Arlene could never have done it.'

'Why not? She'd as much chance as you . . . more.'

'She couldn't, I tell you. She hated—hates—the sight of blood. If she wanted to kill someone, she wouldn't do it that way. That's for sure.'

Silence intervened. Gail sat swilling the remaining coffee in her cup, frowning into it. Remotely, from outside, the sound reached them of the shop door being rattled by a frustrated would-be customer: instinctively, Gail glanced at her watch before eyeing her employer interrogatively, then resigning herself to the situation. She stretched across for Pike's empty cup. The movement roused him.

'See, Gail, the snag is this. I've not got a proper alibi for the night before last. This is where I'm at a disadvantage. I can't prove I wasn't at Gareth's place, at some stage of the proceedings.'

Refilling the cups, she considered the matter. Meanwhile Pike relapsed into apathy. What was he doing, he asked himself drearily, burdening his youthful assistant with his intractable problems? Because she was there, that was why. He had to talk to somebody. Just to think aloud was something of a release. Answers were something else. In all fairness, he couldn't expect those.

'Tell you what,' said Gail, passing the cup back to him. 'Why not say you was with me?'

Pike gaped at her. 'Eh?'

'I can be your alibi.' Her voice rose in excitement. 'I'll say you rang me up that evening to find out if Arlene was over at my place, right? So then I offered to come out with you in the van, to look for her. So you picked me up, say, around midnight and we drove all over town till two. Or whatever time you're not covered for. How about that?'

'They'd check with your parents,' he pronounced, having recovered. 'They'd say you were at home all night.'

'No, they wouldn't. 'Cos I wasn't.'

'How's that again?'

'I was over at my friend Rosemary's,' she said triumphantly. 'We was taping some music and that, and I never left till turned one. Time I got home, my mum and dad had been asleep for hours. I've done it before, quite often. They don't bother to wait up for me any more. So they wouldn't have known if it was before two or after when I come in, see?'

'If you were with Rosemary,' Pike said slowly, 'I couldn't have phoned you at home to ask about Arlene.'

'No problem. We'll say you rang me at Rosemary's. I'll fix it with her. She'll say anything I ask her to. If I tell the cops you called for me in the van and I went off with you, she'll back us up.'

'How about *her* parents?'

'She doesn't live with them. Has her own bedsit. Well? What d'you reckon?'

Planting his cup on a nearby shelf, Pike drummed irresolute fingers on the steel framework. 'How did I know,' he demanded, 'you'd be with Rosemary that evening?'

'Simple. Told you, didn't I, during the day?'

'Why?'

'So as you could reach me if you had to.'

'Why would I need to?'

Gail blinked, as if a scarf had been flapped across her eyes. 'I'm your assistant, aren't I? You like to know where I am after hours, case anything happens at the shop and you've lost your own key. Nothing to it.'

Uneasily, Pike rearranged himself on the box. 'It's a nice offer, Gail. Don't get the idea I'm not grateful. It's only that—'

'Seeing as you like the offer, then take it. I'm quite happy about it.'

'You might not be. If things went wrong.'

'What can go wrong?'

Pike's lips twitched mirthlessly. 'For a start, I could be lying to you, couldn't I? Maybe I did drive over to Gareth's after all.'

'You don't tell fibs, Marvin. I know you better than that.'

Pike said hurriedly, 'There's something we're forgetting. When I was being grilled last night, I never said a word about an alibi. Won't that seem fishy to the Chief?'

'Don't see why.' Gail cogitated. 'All you have to say is

you didn't want to get me involved, only now you're under suspicion you've no choice. Okay?'

'Sounds easy, when you put it like that.' Pike scowled at the concrete floor. 'Another thing. On my way back from cruising around, I called in on my in-laws. If the cops check with them . . .'

'Did they come outside?'

'No. I went in the house for a little while: then I left.'

'I waited outside in the van, then, didn't I? No difficulty there, either.'

His gaze travelled back to her expectant face. 'Gail . . . I really don't know what to say. You'd be setting yourself up, you know. Things could come unstuck.'

She brandished the objection aside. 'Honestly, Marvin, I don't see how it can miss. What if they do keep on about the scissors? They've got no proof.' Pausing, she pondered again. 'I might be able to do somethink about that, too.'

'Do something?' Pike repeated apprehensively.

Gail sprang up. 'I could say I did see Arlene take a pair of them scissors off the rack in the shop last week. That'd take the heat off of you, wouldn't it?'

'Yes, and shove it straight on to her. You realize what you're saying, Gail? We'd virtually be accusing Arlene of killing Gareth.'

'Well, what of it?' A note of defiance had edged into the girl's tone. 'She's the one that's dropped out of sight. If she gets to hear she's under suspicion, it might encourage her to pop up again and put her side of it. If not, she's asking for trouble.' Gail looked at him shiny-eyed. 'Don't you see, Marvin? It'd be passing the buck to her, that's all. Fetch her out of hiding so she can clear her name, or else . . .'

'Or else what?'

'If she never come forward at all,' Gail said breathlessly, 'it could mean somethink else again, couldn't it?'

Pike said faintly, 'Like what?'

'It could mean she really did kill Gareth. What if he was threatening to ditch her or something? P'raps she did do it. If not, what's stopping her from showing herself?'

## CHAPTER 12

'You could have mentioned this before,' Chief Inspector Forester said testily.

'Wasn't to know, was I, I'd be Suspect Number One?'

'Who said you were?'

'Do us a favour, Chief. The way you've had me under the roaster . . .'

'Routine.'

'Oh yes? Questions till midnight? What happens when you really get your knife into somebody?'

'We twist,' Forester said with dour satisfaction. 'And we keep twisting till the flesh parts. Sonny, you've seen nothing yet. Where's this alibi of yours?'

'Waiting outside. Want us to fetch her in?'

'We'll do any fetching, thank you kindly. Before I hear what the young lady has to say, let's recap on what you've just told me. You claim Miss Franklin was with you in the van between about midnight and two a.m.; and she's ready to confirm that you went nowhere near your partner's house in Beech Chase during that time. Right so far?'

'Near enough. I'd say it was after two when I dropped her off.'

'Where was that?'

'Back home, of course.'

'Her parents' home? Not this bedsitter of her friend, Rosemary Someone?'

'At that hour?'

'Would have been a mite inconsiderate,' agreed the chief

inspector. 'More especially as she'd been so quick to abandon their nice cosy evening together in favour of what turned out to be a wild goose chase around the neighbourhood in her employer's van. Why *was* she so willing to join you, by the way?'

'Apart from being an employee, she's a good friend of ours.' The words flowed easily. Pike was starting to respirate again. It was nothing like as thorny as he had feared. 'When she heard Arlene was missing, she was nearly as upset as I was.'

Forester frowned. 'At the time you say you telephoned Miss Franklin,' he remarked, 'your wife could only have been gone a couple of hours. Why the big panic?'

Pike fought the urge to answer swiftly. Instead, he sat back in an attitude of reflection and fixed a sightless gaze upon the wall above the chief inspector's ginger head, from which stance he could record the other's reactions without seeming to notice them. The late morning sunlight was just getting into the room. Warmth was building up. Pike could feel sweat trickling down his neck. It was caused, he knew, by the temperature; not stress. None the less it exasperated him.

'It may not seem a long time to you, Chief. But you've got to remember, she'd—my wife was only supposed to have slipped out for a few minutes to work on the van. In that situation, two hours takes on a different meaning, wouldn't you reckon? Gail saw that, right off. Took it seriously. That's why she came along.'

'Whereas people like me,' Forester suggested blandly, 'are *not* taking it seriously. This what you're saying?'

'For you it's not the same, that's all. You're an outsider. You can't know my wife's habits.'

The chief inspector meditated. 'I'm told,' he murmured presently, 'that one of your wife's habits, as you call them,

in recent months has been to arrive home in the small hours
without apparently sparking any adverse reaction from you.
To my mind, that hardly seems to tie in with—'

'How d'you know?'

'How do I know what?'

'That I never reacted. You don't know what was going
on in my mind.'

'Quite true. I don't.'

Pike stepped back from the edge. 'All I mean is, now and
then it seemed to me these night classes of hers were taking
up too much of her time and energy. I wasn't paranoid
about it.'

'Very forbearing of you,' Forester congratulated him.
'You trusted your wife, in other words?'

'Totally.'

'So what happened to your faith in her, a couple of nights
ago?'

'That,' said Pike, choosing his words and tone of voice
with scrupulous care, 'I've already tried to explain. She
wasn't at night class. She'd come back. She only went out
again to—'

'Yes, I think I've got the picture by now. The one you're
drawing for me. Getting back to the case of Mr Somers,'
added the chief inspector, before Pike could voice an indig-
nant response, 'which is what chiefly engages us at the
moment, I want to take up this matter of the time of death.
Now, you've produced an alibi—or you say you have one
available—for the crucial period between midnight and two
o'clock on the night of the murder. I'll be talking to Miss
Franklin, of course. But even supposing her account stands
up, I must point out to you that we're left with a yawning
gap or two.'

'A gap?'

'Earlier that evening, for example. Between, let's say, ten
o'clock and midnight.'

'I was at home then, wasn't I? Waiting for my wife to come back.'

'So you say.' Forester settled himself comfortably. 'Why should I take your word for it?'

'You don't have to.' Surreptitiously, Pike gripped the edges of his chair. 'Ask the Joneses next door. They'll tell you—'

'We've asked. They can't say for sure.'

'That's ridiculous. I answered the door to—'

'Mrs Jones,' intervened the chief inspector, overriding him without seeming to raise his voice, 'thinks she may have heard faint sounds from your living-room, through the party wall, at about ten-fifteen, ten-thirty. But it could have been the television.'

'I was looking in when my wife came home from the institute.'

'What time did you say that was?'

'A bit after nine-thirty. We had a chat, then she made some ReadyWhip—'

'Yes, you've given us all that. Thereupon she went outside on her famous van-lubricating mission and failed to return. Which left you alone in the house. Correct?'

'Right, but not all the time. I spoke to Alec Jones—twice, in fact. Once on the blower, to ask if they'd seen Arlene or knew where she might have gone. Then again, getting on for midnight, when he called in to—'

'I've heard all this before,' Forester observed, deadpan. 'So?'

'Mr Jones corroborates your story.'

Pike glared at him. 'In that case—'

'He did, certainly, ring at your door and see you. About five or ten minutes to twelve, he estimates. And earlier, he did have a phone call from you. Around a quarter to eleven.'

'Well, then? I couldn't have been—'

'With respect, Mr Pike, it proves nothing about your

actual movements during most of the period we're talking about. You could very well have been over at your partner's house in Beech Chase at some time between—what?—ten o'clock and a quarter to twelve.'

Strolling around to the front of his desk, Forester planted himself squarely upon its metallic edge, folded his arms and regarded Pike from a height. 'Think about it. At ten forty-five or thereabouts, Jones takes a phone call from you. In view of what you tell him, he naturally asumes it comes from next door. But you could just as easily have been calling from your partner's house. Jones has no way of knowing.'

'Garbage. Of course I was—'

'Exactly the same,' pursued Forester remorselessly, 'applies to the several other calls you made that evening, to friends and relatives of your wife. All of them could have originated from Mr Somers's home number.' He lifted a hand, like a Pope. 'I'm not saying they did, mind. I'm saying they could have.'

'You're saying a load of rubbish.' A clamp had descended upon the area between Pike's chest and the base of his throat. It was as much as he could do to eject words: they escaped like half-frozen toothpaste from a tube. 'What's the point of all this? Okay, so I could have made those calls from Gareth's place. I could have made them from New York. I didn't, in fact. I made them from where I live. But so what, anyhow? My partner was rubbed out after midnight, and that's the time when I—'

'Was he?'

Pike's head jolted on his neck. 'Who says he wasn't?'

'Nobody, to my knowledge, has said specifically either way.' Forester spoke on a semi-apologetic note, as if covering for certain inexcusable deficiencies of the investigating squad. From a box on the desk surface behind him he produced an opened pack of slim cigars, withdrew one, proffered it. Pike shook his head. Placing the cigar between his own lips, the chief inspector applied a match and proceeded contemplatively to inhale.

'The fact of the matter is,' he added, reaching behind him again for a battered tin ashtray, 'we're still far from certain just when your partner did . . . meet his end.'

'I thought you could tell. I thought you made tests.'

'Tests aren't conclusive. They're not necessarily that accurate. Numerous factors are involved. The air temperature surrounding the body,' Forester said helpfully, 'being just one of the many, sad to relate. In the case of your partner, things are duly complicated by the fact that he wasn't found slumped in an armchair inside a controlled-heated room, or conveniently tucked up in bed. He was discovered, as you know—'

'I *don't* know. I've not been told.'

'I'm telling you now.' Forester puffed cigar smoke towards the window. 'Mr Somers was found lying on the patio outside his living-room at eleven-fifteen the next morning by a parcels delivery man who couldn't get a reply to his knock at the door. Wanting to make the delivery if he possibly could, he peeped through the front window and saw the patio door flapping in the breeze. Then, when it swung back, he spotted a foot and an ankle just beyond.'

Pike stirred restively. 'I can't see this has anything—'

'In other words, your partner had been sprawled for quite a number of hours on cold flagstones in temperatures ranging from cool in the early hours to warm at daybreak, then hottish during the middle part of the morning. Quite a challenge,' the chief inspector suggested whimsically, 'for any forensic analyst, inspired or otherwise. Our man did quite reasonably, in my opinion. Narrowed it down as much as we could hope.'

'How narrow is that?'

Forester shrugged. 'Taking everything into account, we

can say with some confidence that your partner was dead *prior* to one or two o'clock in the morning. Setting an earlier limit is dodgier. Conceivably, he could have been stabbed at any time after nine the previous evening.' He cocked an eye at Pike. 'See our difficulty?'

'As long as you can see mine. This means I need an alibi for several hours before midnight, as well as after.'

'Quite right.'

'I've given you one from ten onwards. Only you won't accept it.'

Forester flicked ash. 'Because it's not an alibi.'

'What is, then?'

His interrogator eyed the ceiling. 'If you were to produce a witness who was actually with you, at your house—or somewhere else, even—throughout the period in dispute, I'd accept it as proof of your non-involvement. Can you do this?'

'You know I can't.' Pike brandished frustrated arms. 'I've said how I spent that time. If you won't believe me, that's your bad luck.'

'You mean yours, don't you? Let's not forget about the scissors.'

'As if you would.'

'Well, you must admit, you've got some explaining to do. A pair of the same type that stabbed your partner is found inside your van, stained with blood of a group that matches his . . . and you think we'll be inclined to overlook it?'

'No, but you can listen when I say they must have been planted. It's the only explanation that makes sense.'

'Not the only one, surely?'

'See what I mean? You've got it down to me, whatever I tell you. Look,' said Pike, fighting desperation, 'how about fingerprints?'

'None on the scissors. Either the killer wore gloves, or else—'

'I meant at Gareth's place. Doors, windows.'

'Dabs all over the place. We're checking now.'

'You won't find any of 'em are mine. I've not been inside his house since Arlene and I had lunch there, a year or so back. If there's any prints you can't identify, they'll belong to some casual intruder, I'll bet.'

'Someone who got in, you mean, and did the killing?'

'That's right.'

'Using a pair of scissors from your shop display?'

'What makes you so cocksure,' Pike demanded heatedly, 'they came from Margar in the first place, them scissors?' In the fluster of the moment, his verbal grammar was slipping. He knew it, and was furious with himself. Likewise with the chief inspector, whose slight twist of the mouth had betrayed his awareness of Pike's lapse. Let him sneer, he thought. I'll show them. 'They're part of a block consignment from Taiwan, if you want to know. We're not the only shop that stocks them, not by a mile. If you look, you'll find—'

'I'm perfectly willing to accept,' Forester said mildly, 'that I'd find pairs of the selfsame brand all over the country, if I cared to make a search. But how many of them would be likely to carry a Margar price-tag?'

An hour later the chief inspector came back.

'I've talked to Miss Franklin,' he said, re-establishing himself on the desktop. 'She confirms all that you've said about being with you in the van after midnight. Unfortunately . . .'

'I know. Don't tell me. I'm still not covered for earlier.'

'No, but I've remembered something. According to what you've told us, you made a phone call to your partner shortly before midnight to ask whether your wife was there . . .'

'So I did,' Pike put in eagerly. 'That shows Gareth was still alive then, doesn't it?'

'It would, if we had proof of the call. Again, we've only your word for it.' Forester beamed at him. 'Assuming you did make it, though, the question arises—why?'

'Why?'

'What prompted you to contact your partner, at that time?'

'What do you think? I wanted to know if Arlene was with him.'

'But you'd no reason to think she might be. You suspected nothing between them, then. That's what you've told us.'

Pike chewed his lip. 'I'd tried everyone else,' he explained lamely. 'It was all I could think of. I thought maybe they might have had some . . . some business matter to discuss.'

'Over your head? I thought you were the partner, not her.'

'Yes, but . . .'

'In any case,' Forester forged on, 'how did you imagine she could have got there? It's not on any public transport route from your place and she hadn't taken the van. What did you think she'd done—jogged?'

'I reckoned maybe he'd come over in his Merc and picked her up.'

'Just like that? Spur of the moment? Without a word to you?'

'I wasn't thinking it out, at the time. I was getting a bit frantic, don't forget. I just wanted to check.'

'So you checked. All right. Let's assume you're telling me the truth. How long did you talk on the phone, you and your partner?'

'A few minutes.'

'You accepted his denial, of course?'

'I'd no cause not to.'

'Although, when you think about it, your wife could have been standing at his elbow while he was talking.'

Pike subjected the chief inspector to a glare of disfavour.
'I suppose I'd be an idiot to rule it out.'

'Pity we can't trace your wife. Make things a lot easier,
wouldn't it? All sorts of queries she might have the answer
to. As it is,' Forester said regretfully, 'you're the one left in
the hot seat, rather. All the evidence seems to point one way
at the moment, does it not? Just one of those situations, I'm
afraid.'

Pike sat numbly in his chair. He could think of nothing
to say.

'Not,' added his persecutor, 'that we shall leave it at that,
needless to say. We've still quite a few inquiries to make.
Until we've made 'em, I'd like you, Mr Pike, to hold yourself
available, as the jargon has it, and stay closely in touch.
Will you do that for me?'

'Do I have a choice?'

'None whatever,' Forester confirmed cheerfully. 'Should
we need you again at short notice, where can we find you?
At the shop?'

'There, or at home. I shan't be going far.'

The chief inspector smiled. 'I'm glad to hear it.'


CHAPTER 13

'We tried,' said Gail, as they walked back.

Pike made no reply. His mind was busy elsewhere. Active,
but not productive; the more he demanded of it, the less it
supplied. Keeping track of events was becoming increasingly
hard. What had he said? What had he left unsaid? One way
or another, if he hadn't already done so, he was going to
slip up. Then what? Which way could he turn?

Gail was still talking. Something about not being sure the
Chief had believed her. Pike was familiar with the feeling.

He was beginning to doubt his own veracity, even in those instances where he had believed previously that he was telling the truth. Herein lay the danger. The line between reality and fiction was starting to blur.

As they approached the shop, something Gail said got through to him. 'When will you be getting the van back?'

'They're still holding it for tests,' he said morosely. 'I told him I needed it for the business, but I might as well have saved my breath.'

'I expect we can do without it for a day or two.' Gail's manner was abstracted; she was glancing behind her, wrinkling her nose a little as she surveyed the parade. Waiting for him to unlock the door, she continued to look back the way they had come, as if half-expecting to see an oncoming horde of irate shoppers brandishing Government leaflets relating to retail opening hours. In fact, few people were about. It was midway through the lunch-hour and the parade was almost deserted, quietly soaking up the heat. Gaining admittance to the shop, Pike held the door for her while presenting the OPEN sign to the street and sniffing the aroma of tobacco and confectionery and newsprint that invariably hit his nostrils as he entered his domain. For an instant, he felt that he was back in the real world, the one he knew about, liberated from the fantasy sphere in which he had been cloistered. The feeling ebbed. The nightmare was still about him. Making mechanically for the counter, he switched on the till and rearranged a few newspapers. Joining him, Gail produced from a plastic carrier bag the twin takeaway cartons of chicken and chips that she had secured after they left the police station. She placed them alongside the toffee display. Pike eyed them with repulsion.

'If you want to have yours in peace, at the back . . .'

'You must eat some yourself,' she said severely. Opening one of the cartons, she pushed one under his nose before retiring with the other to a stool behind the counter. 'Anybody that don't fancy the smell,' she announced through a mouthful, 'can push off and come back later.'

Resting his spine against the wall-shelving, Pike did his best. He had no great success. Gail said, 'You've got to keep your strength up, Marvin. No sense in starving, is there?'

'Might solve a few problems.' He stared at the free-standing display racks at the centre of the shop floor.

Observing the direction of his gaze, Gail said, 'The Chief asked about the scissors.'

'What did you tell him?'

'Same as what you did, probably. He was going on about the price-tag. Okay, I said, so they come off our rack, the ones they found in the van. But how do we know who took 'em? Anybody could've, couldn't they?'

'Try convincing him.'

'Some light-fingered customer. A kid, even. Not the sort of thing they normally lift, but one of 'em might have just fancied a pair. Present for his mum or something.'

Gail severed a strip of chicken flesh from the bone with her front teeth. 'What I don't see,' she concluded, 'is how anyone can say it must've been you. Nobody can prove it.'

Pike felt faintly stirred. 'I don't see how they can prove it was the pair that was used, either.'

She looked up at him doubtfully. 'The blood . . .'

'Common group, the Chief says. Could be sheer coincidence,'

'Finding 'em in the van, though. That's what must look funny to the Fuzz.'

'Hilarious,' Pike said gloomily. 'Not that the Chief laughs a lot. He seems to reckon . . .' He looked at Gail across the counter. 'You didn't tell him anything? About Gareth, I mean, and the accounts?'

'Never said a word,' she protested. 'You told us not to. I

wouldn't let you down, Marvin. You need someone to stand
up for you. If there's anything else you want me to do,
you've only got to say.'

Pike was touched. Nobody had ever before spoken to him
like this. The idea crossed his mind that Gail in some
extraordinary way had fallen for him and was now pursuing
the path of blind devotion; a moment's reflection, however,
was enough to scotch the theory. Modern youngsters like
Gail didn't succumb to the dubious magnetism of under-
weight, balding shop-owners with trading problems. The
supportiveness she was showing stemmed palpably from a
basic sense of employee loyalty; nothing more. Which made
it no less acceptable. 'Thanks, Gail,' he said humbly. 'I
appreciate that. But I shan't be asking you for anything
else. You've done enough already.'

'Don't seem to have achieved much, though, do I?' she
said despondently. 'I mean, I tried my best to convince the
Chief I did come out with you in the van, and I think he
sort of believed me . . . only he didn't seem that interested.
Didn't seem to reckon it was important.'

'He doesn't.'

Gail blinked. 'Why not?'

'Because apparently it's possible Gareth was stabbed a
good while before midnight.'

'How could he have been?'

'They can't always tell the exact time of death. The
temperature—'

'No. I meant, you phoned him, didn't you, when it
was getting on for twelve? If he was alive then, how
could . . .'

Her voice tailed off as a middle-aged man with a yellow
Labrador on a leash came in and asked for cigarettes.
'Naafi-break?' he enquired jovially. 'Sorry to muscle in on
the party, but I'm desperate. Filter-tips, if you don't mind.
Down, Shep! You can't have other people's lunch.'

'Yes, he can.' Pike handed across the plastic carton of chicken remnants. 'I've had all I want.'

'Very kind of you, squire. Shep, you're in luck. Have to take out the bones, but there's a fair bit of flesh we can salvage. You're sure? Well, thanks a lot.' Whistling like a demented sheepdog handler, the man made off in a whirl of canine limbs, leaving Gail to gaze accusingly at Pike.

'You should've eaten it all yourself.'

'What I had was too much.'

'It's all that chief inspector's fault. Harassing you, that's what he's doing. Mind you . . .' Gail paused, looking embarrassed. 'In a way, I can see his point. He's only got your word for it, hasn't he, that you rang Gareth and spoke to him? If only Arlene could've been there to back you up . . . But then if she had been, you wouldn't have rung in the first place, would you? Talk about a mess-up.'

'What I need,' Pike said hopelessly, 'is another witness. Somebody to say they heard me making the call.'

'I'll do it,' she offered.

Decisively he shook his head. 'Wouldn't work. You've come forward once—if you did it again, the Chief'd just laugh at you. Besides, I don't want you getting yourself too involved. You could end up in a real scrape.'

'I'm not bothered. How about someone,' she said thoughtfully, 'that could tell the police they was with you at home all evening, up till midnight? Them neighbours of yours—the Joneses. Can't they help?'

'They've given me all the assistance I can do with,' Pike said drily.

'And there's nobody else?'

'Who's going to lie their heads off and maybe land in jail for my benefit? I'm not some Mafia godfather. I don't *know* anyone.'

Scowling towards the window, Gail said, 'You can see what's bugging the Chief. Unsupported testimony. That's what it's called. Unsupported testimony. There *must* be some other witness we can rake up.'

Pike regarded her attentively. 'Tell me honestly, Gail. Does it bug you?'

She looked back at him, puzzled. 'How d'you mean?'

'Would it make you feel happier if you knew for a fact that I *was* at home, up until midnight?'

'You don't have to ask us that, Marvin. I've said, haven't I? It's obvious, you couldn't have—'

'You may think it's obvious. But you could be biased, you know.' He was speaking recklessly now, giving free rein to his tongue, barely estimating the consequences. 'What if I could prove it to you?'

'If you can prove it to me, you can prove it to the Chief.' Gail, for the first time, was eyeing him with a certain reserve. The sight of it maddened Pike. He lost his head.

'I *can* prove it, you know,' he shouted. 'I do have a witness.'

The girl's lips parted, closed, parted again. 'You serious? I thought you was saying—'

'Never mind what I was saying. If you want me to show you, I will. I can't keep it to myself any longer. I have to show somebody.'

'Show them what, Marvin?' She spoke with a mature kindliness that took him off balance. 'You can tell me. I'm on your side, remember.'

'No need to take sides,' he muttered, fumbling for a handkerchief to wipe his face. This time he couldn't blame the summer heat alone. The moistness of his skin was due primarily to an inner stress that had been building relentlessly within him and had now exploded with devastating force. 'Just let me take you there. Have a look for yourself.'

'Take us where? I don't get it, Marvin.' She spoke a little fearfully. 'Who's this witness you're talking about?'

Seizing her wrist, he yanked her off the stool. 'You'll see,' he said.

Keeping pace at his side, Gail said puffingly, 'Didn't you tell the Chief you'd be at the shop if he wanted you?'

'If he wants me, he'll have to wait.'

She glanced around. 'I know this part. Isn't Beech Chase somewhere near here?'

'Next on the left,' Pike confirmed.

'Not making for Gareth's house, are you? Might still be full of coppers.'

'We're not making for the house.'

Trotting a few steps to catch up, Gail accompanied him in a baffled silence to the next turning. Even in daylight, Beech Chase remained an esoteric environment. In addition to a superabundance of trees that tended to blot out the sky, its entire length was bordered on both sides by screens of lower but even denser foliage—holly bushes, rhododendrons, blackthorn—between road and footways, so that the houses lurking to the rear seemed to belong elsewhere, claim no connection with their nominal address. The end of the thoroughfare from which they were approaching lay in peace, undisturbed as yet by the march of the excavators and the pipes. Pike had chosen this way to avoid passing the coach-house. Ahead of them loomed the entrance to the side drive. As they reached it, he placed a hand against Gail's shoulder and propelled her round, gestured her along the track.

She half-turned to him. 'What if anybody—'

'We're out for an afternoon stroll, okay? Or we're visiting someone at the big house. Leave any talking to me.'

From somewhere further along the road they had just left, a roaring note started up, suggesting the operation of heavy mechanical plant. The noise came as a timely boost to Pike's backbone. It would not have taken much, he sensed, to impel him out of the track and back along the street to the sanctuary of the humbler district through which they had come. His return to the coach-house garden was proving a more traumatic experience than he had reckoned upon. For Gail's sake, however, he had to retain a semblance of assurance. She was a plucky kid to follow him this far. He mustn't let her down.

Impulsively he halted and gripped her by the arms. She let out a small yip of alarm. 'It's all right,' he said soothingly. 'I only want to tell you something. Come in here a minute.'

He drew her aside into a natural recess formed by a semi-circle of shrubs. 'I want you to listen for a bit. I want to explain what happened.'

'Go ahead then, Marve.' Her attempt to persevere with the easy familiarity she had always cultivated was a pathetic flop: plainly she was terrified. He resumed a little impatiently.

'I couldn't tell the Chief, see. He'd never have understood. Not like you, Gail. You're on my side, aren't you?'

'That's it, Marve. I'm with you, all the way.'

'You're not just saying that?'

''Course not. I want to help.'

'Listen, then. You've got to understand about Arlene. The night she disappeared . . . we did have a dust-up. I misled everyone on that.'

Gail's eyes widened as they stared into his. 'Go on.'

'It wasn't *about* anything. She just got mad because I asked for something to eat. That's all it was, to be quite honest with you. Just for wanting a meal, I got on the wrong side of her and she flipped. She'd always hated me eating. Seemed to reckon it was vulgar or something.'

'Silly.' Gail's voice was faint.

'She couldn't help it. Just the way she was made. I used to humour her,' he explained. 'Cook for myself, half the time. That evening she wouldn't let me. Said she'd just cleaned the cooker and wasn't having it gummed up again. I told her I'd boil myself an egg—just a lousy boiled egg. She still said no. Stood in my way when I tried to get to the burner.'

'She must've been bonkers,' declared Gail, jolted into garrulity.

'I've wondered about that. Anyway I was hungry, so I tried to shift her aside so I could reach the cooker. She wouldn't budge. Just stood there, holding me off. So I lost my cool.'

'I'm not surprised.'

'I wanted that egg and I was damn well going to have it. To be quite honest with you, Gail, when she took that attitude it was more than I could do to keep a grip on myself. For once, I blew my top. I did handle her a bit roughly, I'll admit that. Got her to one side and held her there while I switched on the burner.'

'Did she struggle?'

'Well, this is the point. She—'

Pike paused. The noise of machinery from the street had died suddenly, leaving a silence that seemed to permeate every leaf and twig that hung about them. Mechanically he glanced at his watch. 'Three-thirty,' he commented. 'Tea-break. Quiet, isn't it? Reminds me of when I was here before.'

Gail looked back at him. 'When was that, Marvin?'

'Don't rush me,' he said tetchily. 'I want to get the sequence right . . . What was I saying?'

'Holding on to Arlene.'

'Holding on to Arlene. I hadn't realized, you know, how strong she was. She may not have turned the scale at much, but this course of hers—handling wrenches and suchlike—must have done something for her muscle. Any rate, she came right back at me and caught me off balance. I fell against the fridge and bashed my head on the door handle.'

Pike dabbed at his head. 'Knocked me half-silly for a minute. Then before I knew what was happening, she had me by the throat.'

'Choking you, like?'

'She would have. I couldn't get my breath and she was just hanging on, her face was all twisted ... To be quite honest with you, Gail, I was scared. I thought she was out of her mind. I stretched my hands out and managed to grab her. So there was the two of us, clinging on like a couple of maniacs and neither of us saying a word. I don't think I knew what I was doing, hardly.'

'You had to protect yourself.'

'This is all I was thinking of, at the time. Self-defence, you might say. I wasn't keen to be strangled. So I didn't dare let go till she started loosening her hands. When she did, I took mine away. But instead of stopping where she was, she kind of slid down on to the floor and landed in a heap.'

'Oh, my.'

'At first I thought she was fooling around. Then when she never moved, even when I tried to help her up, I started to get panicky.'

'What did you do?'

'For a while, I couldn't think what to do. She was sort of bunched up on the tiles and I couldn't seem to straighten her out. I tried getting brandy into her but it just came back out of her mouth. So then I had to face up to it.'

Gail blinked several times.

Pike peered at her. 'You do understand what I'm telling you?'

'I ... I think so, Marvin.'

'You can see what led up to it? The way she brought it on herself?'

''Course I can.' After an interval, Gail added in a whisper, 'Where is she now, Marvin? What did you do with her?'

Taking possession of her arm, Pike steered her out from the shelter of the shrubs. 'Like I said, I want to show you.'

At the spot alongside the fence, some evidence of disturbance remained. To the observant eye, there could be no mistaking the traces of recent upheaval. He had made, Pike saw, almost too good a job of achieving this effect. Now, he was in a fever to repair the damage. He nodded at the rectangle of ground.

'Arlene's there.'

Gail stood looking. Her speechlessness caused Pike no amazement: it was only what he had anticipated. He didn't like what he was doing to the girl, but there had been no alternative: he'd had to confide in someone, spread the burden. And now that the step had been taken, he was experiencing a sense of release bordering upon euphoria. Perhaps, after all, a way existed out of this maze. It had to.

'Fetch us that branch, will you? The one lying over there. And find one for yourself.'

From where they stood, the coach-house was invisible, hidden by the intervening foliage that occupied much of the garden's air-space. Despite their seclusion, Pike spoke in an undertone and Gail, when she responded, did so in the same way. 'What do we want branches for?'

'To sweep the leaves across,' he said impatiently. 'Can't you see how it shows up? I want that centre part levelled, where it drops. Get the idea?'

'Listen . . .' Gail gulped and swallowed. 'Listen, Marvin. If Arlene's buried there, don't you think we should tell the Chief? He still thinks she's just gone missing. He's got a right to—'

Pike said brutally, 'Either you're with me, Gail, or you're a hostile witness as far as I'm concerned. It's for you to choose.'

'I'm with you, Marvin. You know that. It's only—'

'Lend us a hand, then. We've not much time.'

'Slightly off target, Pike, I'm sorry to say. You've no time left at all.'

The voice boomed from the direction of the gate. Wheeling, Pike met the united inspection of Chief Inspector Forester, his assistant Joe, and a pair of uniformed constables stationed by the toolshed. The expressions of all four of them conveyed a kind of insolent phlegmatism that had the effect of rousing him to fury. He took a stride or two towards them.

'Very smart,' he bawled, shaking a fist in true melodramatic fashion. 'A neat bit of shadow work, I suppose you'd call that. I hope the ratepayers appreciate it. How much did it cost you?'

'A little inconvenience,' Forester replied mildly. 'Half a gallon of petrol. Nothing too damaging. Thinking about a spot of gardening, Pike?'

'A spot of peace and quiet, that's all we were after. But you can't get away from it, can you? Take an afternoon walk, all you get is people crowding you, trying to prove they're macho or something. What's wrong? Afraid I might do a bunk?'

'Not afraid, just curious.'

'What about?'

'Why you should choose to come here for an after-lunch stroll—and bring Miss Franklin. Not exactly the happiest of destinations, I'd have thought.'

'Where we make for is our business.'

'It's mine, too, when I've asked you to be available.' The chief inspector sauntered across, trailed by Joe, who extended a foot to stir experimentally the mulch strewn loosely about the area. 'And I still don't see,' added Forester, studying his deputy's activity, 'what lures either of you to a spot like this. With so much countryside to choose from.'

'Miss Franklin came because I asked her to. I wanted to

show her where my partner lived, before the place was
flogged off to some ghoul chasing a quick profit.'

'How touching. But your partner didn't live here, I take
it, at the end of the garden? What's the big attraction of ten
square yards of leaf-mould?'

Pike glanced from the chief inspector to Joe, then at the
toolshed, then at Gail. He shrugged. 'Have it your way,' he
said, in the monotone of unconditional surrender. 'I can't
take any more. I've had it. We were just on our way over
to you anyhow, Chief. Miss Franklin reckoned I should tell
you, so that's what I'd decided to do.'

'Tell me what?'

'That my wife's buried here. It's the honest truth. No
deception. Plain statement of the facts.' Pike sat abruptly
on a tree-stump, thrust back the few remaining strands of
his hair, massaged his eyes for a moment or two and then
looked up. 'How does that grab you, Chief Inspector?'

Forester swapped glances with Joe, who was scratching
his head. 'I'd be more impressed,' he said frankly, 'but for
one tiny thing.'

Apprehension clutched Pike. 'Yes? What might that be?'

'Nothing to speak of. Merely the fact that all our exca-
vations to date have turned up nothing whatever.' The chief
inspector's tone hardened. 'There's no trace of your wife's
body, this end of the garden or anywhere else. Just what
have you done with her, Pike?'

# CHAPTER 14

After a few hours, Pike found, the yellow-emulsioned walls
of the interview room began to exert a hypnotic influence of
their own, as if vying with the endeavours of Chief Inspector
Forester and his henchmen to break him into small, easily-

handled pieces that could be examined at leisure for deficiencies and flaws.

Each time he was left alone, the paintwork took over. Its
scrutiny was inescapable. And yet, whenever he lifted his
head, there was nothing tangible to be seen. It was almost
a relief when the human element came back. At least, then,
he had someone to talk to.

'Didn't I mention it?' The sardonic phrase was becoming
a habit, an antidote to his insecurity. Outside, darkness was
assembling. How much could a fellow take, for how long?
'I accidentally choked her, then I got scared. I took her over
in the van to Gareth's place and buried her there. I was
hoping she'd be found and he'd get the blame.'

'You did mention it, yes. Thirty times, or thereabouts.
It's a good story, Pike, but it's not borne out by the
facts.'

'I dropped her wedding ring, for God's sake, half way up
the path. Didn't you find that, either?'

Forester snapped on the light. The walls flinched, looked
sicklier than ever. 'We found that, all right. Quite early on,
as it happens, in the course of a routine search of the premises
and grounds. Which also accounts for our discovery of
that patch of disturbed earth by the end fence, if you want
to know.'

'There's just one thing I want to know, Chief, right now.
What's become of my wife? Where is she?'

'I'm waiting for you to tell me.'

'How can I? I'm as much in the dark as you are.'

'You'll have to forgive me,' said Forester, with resort to
heavy irony, 'if I find that hard to stomach. You buried her
there, after all, in the first place. You've assured us of that.
She's not there now, so what did she do in the meantime?
Rise up and walk?'

'I don't think that's in very good taste, Chief Inspector.'

'Believe it or not, I'm putting it forward as a serious

proposition. You're quite sure she was actually dead when you dug her in?'

Pike stared at him. 'I . . . Of course I'm sure. She'd been laid out for hours. I was humping her around and she never twitched a muscle. Of course she was dead.'

'There have been cases,' Forester murmured, 'where corpses have returned to life literally from the grave. I'm not saying this is one of them, but you can't rule it out.'

'She'd have suffocated when I buried her.'

'Not necessarily. Air pockets.'

'What?'

'There could have been just enough oxygen around her face to keep her going for a few minutes after you left. You didn't hang about, I take it?'

'Would you have?'

'And you didn't inter her that deeply, I imagine. Since the idea was for us to find her and point the finger at Mr Somers.'

'I doubt if she was more than a couple of inches under.'

'There you are, then. If she suddenly regained consciousness and managed to struggle free . . .'

'It's crazy.'

'Crazier things are on record.'

'If something like that happened,' blurted Pike after an interval for thought, 'why hasn't she turned up?'

The chief inspector settled back. 'One or two explanations occur to me. She might have lost her memory. Hardly astonishing if she had. In which case she could have gone wandering off and be living rough somewhere, hiding out with hippies, junkies—any number of possibilities. Then again, she might have gone under cover on purpose.'

'Why would she want to do that?'

'To get back at you, of course. According to your story, you'd manhandled her. I know, I know: you never intended to kill her. But you'd gone for her—shall we agree on that?

Therefore, what more natural than a thirst for revenge? Vanish for a week or two, let you sweat it out, put you through purgatory. Isn't this what she might have decided?'

'You're the expert. You seem to know about these things.'

'But you know your wife, presumably. You think she might have been capable of such a course of action?'

Pike rested the back of his head tiredly against the wall. 'If it's revenge we're talking about, I reckon my case is just as strong as hers, if not stronger.'

'That doesn't answer my question.'

'I'm sick of answering your questions.'

'Tough cheese, because I've more for you. If you're dismissing my theory, Pike, as you seem to be, do you by any chance have one of your own to offer? If so, I'd be intrigued to hear it.'

'You wouldn't, you know.'

Unzipping his eyelids, Pike aimed his gaze at the door, which was similar to one he had seen on a recent TV crime series, down to the small pane of steel-meshed glass let into the upper part of the panel. He strove to recall the style of dialogue used in the episodes. Fast, clipped, witty. The brand of verbal give-and-take that was, he knew, beyond his capabilities. In real life, conversations had a knack of working out less slickly than they did on a typewriter. Keep it simple.

'Far as you're concerned,' he continued, 'my guess, Chief, is that you'd sooner stick with your original idea. Not the one about Arlene climbing out of her own coffin. I mean the one that has me dodging over to Gareth's place that night, catching them at it and putting the snuffers on both of 'em. Right?'

For a moment Forester was silent. 'You've got to admit,' he said eventually, scanning his fingernails, 'it's the one that best fits the situation.'

'I'm not making any admissions. Let me ask you something, Chief, by way of a change. Regarding my partner, who's to say he wasn't attacked and done for by a total stranger . . . some intruder?'

'We rule nothing out,' Forester said tonelessly. 'We keep open minds.'

Dimly encouraged, Pike went on. 'Plush district, that, wouldn't you say? Easy pickings. Break-in figures must be smashing all records, from what you read.'

'Statistics,' the chief inspector acknowledged, 'fail to indicate a reduction in the area, sad to say.'

'Okay, then. What if somebody around here knew that Gareth had a stake in a shop. A customer,' Pike added on a note of sudden inspiration. 'Somebody who calls in regularly. They could have got to know Gareth's address and figured there'd be stuff there to pinch. And the same customer,' he concluded, coming forward to plant both elbows on the interview table, 'could have palmed the scissors. Simple as that.'

'Too simple. It wouldn't account for the scissors finding their way into your van.'

'If this customer knew about Gareth, he could just as easily know about me. Where I live, where the van's kept . . . The lot.'

'Interesting hypothesis,' said Forester, sounding bored.

'There's another possibility. The workmen.'

'Workmen?'

'The pipe-layers outside. They've been operating along Beech Chase for weeks. They could well have picked up any amount of local colour. What's to have stopped one of 'em —more than one, maybe—paying my partner a visit that night, aiming to clean him out?'

'Nothing.'

'You been grilling them?'

'No.'

'For Christ's sake!' Pike threw himself back. 'You admit

it could have happened that way, and yet at the same time—'

'What you're forgetting, Pike, is that there were no signs of forcible entry into the house. If outsiders had been involved, don't you think there would have been?'

'I'm not paid to think along those lines. I'm simply pointing out—'

'Everything, so far, suggests that whoever was there with Mr Somers that night was known to him. Somebody he'd no cause to be afraid of.'

'But supposing—'

'No shattered panes, remember. No burst locks. No signs of a struggle. Whoever called on him, your partner must have opened the door and let them in, and up until the fatal moment he was arguably in no fear for his safety.' Forester paused to examine the ceiling. 'That's our reading of events, at any rate.'

Pike's shoulders slumped. 'In that case, why not just go ahead and charge me? Get it over with. Why fool around?'

'Open minds, Pike.' Forester tapped the side of his head significantly. 'We prefer a case to be clear-cut. This one's still fuzzy. Can't we sharpen it up a little?'

'I've nothing more to say.'

'I think you might have.' The chief inspector gazed at him dreamily. 'I'm waiting.'

'They've not charged you yet, then?'

Pike flapped a hand. 'As good as. Chief says he's got some more inquiries to make, but I reckon he's just having a bit of a game. He gets a kick out of it.'

'He's rotten,' Gail said hotly. 'So he reckons you did it?'

'Did what? Suffocated Arlene or stabbed Gareth? Or both? I don't know what he thinks. I'm not sure he knows himself.'

Gail took a restless turn about the room. 'My dad says,

have you got a solicitor? He knows one that's quite good.
My Uncle Ernie had him when he was claiming for a broken
leg and he reckoned he was mustard. We could ask him
if—'

'Thanks, but I've got this bloke of my own. Handled all
the business start-up for me and Gareth. If I need a lawyer
I'll be in touch with him.'

'It's not a matter of *if*. You ought to have someone now.'

Pike said absently, 'I'll think about it.'

The girl studied him worriedly. 'You got to stick around
here till they decide?'

'Nobody tells me anything.' Pike surveyed the first-floor
room of the police station to which he had been taken, before
stealing another glance at her. 'To be quite honest with you,
I'm surprised they let you come up here and see us. What
did you do—shove on half a pint of scent and loosen your
blouse?'

She gave him a small, embarrassed smile. 'Just hung
around till they got sick of the sight of me. In the end the
desk sergeant said I could have five minutes, only to keep
out of the Chief's way or there might be ructions. He's not
bad, that one. Quite sympathetic, really. Reckons I'm your
fiancée.'

Pike sniffed. 'What makes him think that?'

'I suppose he just took it for granted, like.' The girl
paused. 'Didn't mind, Marvin, did you? Me coming to see
you, I mean? I wasn't sure—'

'Makes no odds,' he muttered, nibbling at a knuckle. 'Not
a lot you can do for us.'

'The time I could've done something,' she said forlornly,
'was earlier on today.'

Pike's attention was captured. 'Why? What could you
have done?'

'On our way back to the shop, I noticed somebody following us. I should have said something.'

'Copper?'

'They was keeping an eye on you, wasn't they? The whole time. This is why they showed up in Gareth's garden when you was . . . when you was . . .'

'What's the difference?' Pike snorted. 'One way or another, the Chief was out to nail me for Gareth. Now he reckons he's got me for Arlene, so that's a bonus. Okay— her I'm responsible for. I admit that, even though it was an accident. Gareth—no way. I'm not taking the rap for that.'

'I should hope not. And as far as Arlene's concerned,' Gail said thoughtfully, 'they still can't accuse you of nothing, to my way of thinking. I mean, she wasn't there, was she? She's still missing. So how can they say you did anythink to her?'

'They'll think of something. The Chief will.'

'That's *daft!* You stick up for yourself, Marvin. Don't let them put one over on you. Listen, you want to know what I think?'

'I figure you're going to tell me,' Pike said resignedly.

Gail was undeterred. 'I reckon I was right in the first place. It was Arlene stabbed Gareth with them scissors. I know, but listen. What if you never had that bust-up with her—never strangled her? What if it was just all in your head?'

He gaped at her. 'You telling me I'm barmy or something?'

''Course not. But it can happen, you know. People can dream things. It might've been something you sort of wanted to do, underneath like, so when you woke up after dreaming about it you thought it had really happened. What d'you say to that?'

Pike felt that his eyebrows had been gummed to his hairline. 'I dunno,' he said faintly. 'It seemed real enough at the time . . .'

'Dreams often do.' Gail's theorizing gathered pace. 'What

with Arlene disappearing and that, it's not surprising. But you can see what I'm getting at? Arlene's not buried in that garden now—'cos she never was. What happened was that she went over to the house, had a fight with Gareth—p'raps he was going to ditch her, something like that—killed him with the scissors, then went back to your place to plant them in the van. Then took off. Now she's lying low somewhere, waiting for you to be accused of Gareth's murder. In other words,' Gail concluded jubilantly, 'you've been set up. Obvious, isn't it? It's the only explanation that fits.'

Pike experienced momentary breathlessness. 'It's true,' he puffed, 'I was under a lot of stress that evening. Things might have got on top of me. Maybe it *was* a nightmare.'

'Now you're talking, Marve. At least, you should be—to the Chief Inspector. Tell him what you think may have happened.'

'Mind you,' Pike said slowly, 'it could cut both ways.'

'What could?'

'What we've just been saying. All right, maybe I did dream about Arlene. I'm not saying it's impossible. Only, in that case, I could just as easily have dreamt about Gareth, couldn't I?'

Gail looked at him in bafflement. 'Don't get you. Gareth's dead. They found his body.'

'Exactly. And I could have been responsible. I could have killed him in a sort of nightmare and then forgotten about it, same as you forget dreams when you wake up.' Pike gestured feebly. 'Either way, I'm in no position to argue. Can't confirm or deny, can I? Heads they win, tails I lose. The situation's impossible.'

# CHAPTER 15

Midway through a meal of beefburger and chips which Pike hadn't wanted, hadn't asked for, could barely stomach and was consuming mainly to help pass the time, he received another visit from the chief inspector.

'More questions?' he inquired. 'Reckoned you might have done for the night, but life's full of surprises.'

'Once you've reasoned that out,' Forester said solemnly, 'you're on the road to no longer being taken aback by any of it. For example. If I were to tell you to get your jacket on and come with me outside to a waiting patrol car for a short ride . . . would that strike you as unexpected?'

'No. Just a flaming nuisance.'

'Settled in here, are you? Reluctant to leave?'

'Neither, frankly. Only I get this feeling that whatever it is you have in mind won't rate as an improvement. Correct me,' Pike added generously, 'if I'm wrong.'

'It's all a matter of opinion.' The chief inspector slid the canteen plate neatly to one side. 'Suppose we discuss it as we go along?'

In the car, Pike was introduced to another of Forester's assistants, an inspector this time. He seemed young to have achieved such a rank. Hardly a day older than himself, Pike calculated, and with a fresh, ingenuous air about him more suited to a new arrival at a theological college. His name was Cliff Morgan. 'Hails from South Wales, does Cliff,' the chief inspector said informatively, 'and he's got a tongue to match. Don't try to out-talk him, is my advice. You'll live to regret it.'

Inspector Morgan grinned. 'I'm willing to give a fair

hearing to anybody,' he remarked. 'As long as they don't try to contradict me. I don't take disputation kindly, seeing as I'm invariably right.'

Forester jerked his chin. 'See what I mean?'

The atmosphere inside the Rover seemed suspiciously matey. Pike couldn't decide what to make of it. He was being treated almost as one of the boys. Between the two detectives there was no formality or constraint of any kind: they might have been brothers, out on a family jaunt. Out of the blue, Pike found himself wishing he had been blessed with a sibling. One older than himself, a wise head to consult, a prop in times of earthquake. In addition to their other, innumerable shortcomings, Pike thought with a touch of bitterness, his parents had blandly deprived him of this benefit, into the bargain. Some people were born to misfortune.

'All set up?' Forester asked the inspector as the car nosed at a sedate pace towards the ring road. The driver was a uniformed youngster of stoical demeanour and no words. Pike had not been introduced to him.

Forming a circle with thumb and forefinger, Morgan ran it over an imaginary peg in mid-air. 'No movement, though, as yet. Lashings of time. Still coming up to ten-thirty. Good dark evening, no moon.'

'Heavy,' observed the chief inspector, running a finger around his collar.

'Sticky,' agreed his deputy. 'They say we're in for a blazing August. We'll see. I've my holidays coming up in two weeks, remember? That usually does it. Weather'll change, you'll see, the day before I'm due to go. Never fails. Pity crime's not as predictable.'

'The amount is,' growled Forester.

'Did I tell you, by the bye? I'd a job persuading Plymstock to take me seriously, at first. Thought he was being conned into something, I imagine. Wasn't until the Super had a

private word with him, eyeball to eyeball so to speak, that
he cottoned on, agreed to cooperate. I get this,' Morgan
complained equably, 'all the way along the line. If one only
had some extra authority to chuck around . . .'

'You could try sprouting a beard.'

The young inspector shook his head. 'Nobody can spot
your whiskers at the far end of a telephone. What I need to
be able to do is to pull rank.'

'I've put my modest word in for you,' Forester assured
him. 'Can't do more.'

Unreasonably irked by this conversation of dubious
relevance, Pike said, 'Where exactly are we making for?'

Having taken a left turn, the driver was steering them
into patchily-lit terrain that to Pike was far from unfamiliar.
He had scarcely needed to pose the query; his intention had
been to bring the dialogue back to a level at which he could
join in. He had little success, although Inspector Morgan
went so far as to peer through the side window in a vague
quest for orientation. 'Not far now. Take it easy, Bruce boyo.
Watch out for the rubble-heaps. Spending the ratepayers'
money like water, they are, hereabouts, and we don't want
to add to the financial burden, do we, by wrecking the car?
Wouldn't do at all.'

Pike had half-guessed it from the start. It had always
been on the cards that they would bring him here, preferably
at night. Reconstruction, it was called. He had read Press
accounts of numerous instances. Quite often, it seemed,
some lookalike policewoman was pressed into the role of
victim, togged up to match, paraded for the media's benefit.
Did results ever follow? Nothing ever seemed to be said
about that. A frisson of fear trickled through Pike. Surely
they weren't planning to make him hoist a dummy replica
of Arlene shoulder-high, bury the corpse all over again? He
would refuse. He'd a right to. Nobody could force him.

To the driver, Forester said calmly, 'Thirty yards or so

past the drive. There's a space on the verge, behind a holly bush. Tuck in there.'

Taking the car into a U-turn, the driver chuntered it back to the spot, reversed into the gap. Part of the view was blocked by holly leaves, but the nearside occupants of the vehicle—Inspector Morgan in front, and Pike to his rear— could see along the barely-illuminated street as far as the coach-house, the façade of which lay in darkness although faintly silhouetted by such light as there was from nearby lamps. Switching off his lights and motor, the driver settled back in his seat. The others did the same. Nothing more was said.

Mystification overtook Pike. What kind of wacky game was this? Who was Plymstock when he was at home? Adjusting position cautiously, he peered through the gloom at the outline of Forester, sunk into the upholstery on the offside of the car with his chin resting on his neck.

'I don't know what this is meant to prove, but to be quite honest with you, Chief, there's nothing more I can tell you. You've had the lot.'

'Could be a long wait,' remarked Morgan from the front, rearranging himself more comfortably. 'I'd find myself a good position, boyo, if I were you, and stick to it.'

Pike glared at the back of the seat. 'Makes no odds if we're here all night. You'll get no more out of me, I'm telling you.'

Forester said lazily, 'Nod off to sleep, then, if you want. We'll see you don't miss anything.'

Notwithstanding the warmth of the night, it became cramped and a shade chilly inside the car. Pike's circulation was poor and he suffered from clammy feet. Wriggling his toes strenuously, with little to show for it, he stretched and compressed himself by turns, put his head back, tried to doze, thrust it forward, tried to stay awake. All the time, he was acutely and angrily aware of the semi-slumped forms of his three companions, each contributing body-odour to the car's interior while detracting from the space available. He itched to say something, to fracture the nerve-jangling silence. Each time he tried, courage deserted him.

This, he reflected grimly, was not what he had always understood by the phrase *Helping the police*. Was it legal? Gail had been right: he should have consulted a solicitor, straight off. Then he would have been advised of his rights. Not crouched here, listening to the lung-movements of three guardians of the law. What in hell were they waiting for?

A solitary pedestrian passed them. A male figure, just discernible in the near-darkness, his shoe-leather scuffing the loose pebbled surface of the footway. Pike tracked his progress. At a point some distance to their rear, the pedestrian turned into a gateway, paused, seemed to look back at the motionless car, then passed through, out of earshot. In the renewed silence, Inspector Morgan spoke sleepily.

'He'll be lifting the receiver just about . . . now. An alert resident, dutifully reporting a suspicious occurrence. No doubt he's a member of Neighbourhood Watch.'

Forester stirred. 'I trust our esteemed desk sergeant digested his briefing?'

'Did my best to make it clear.'

'Because if he didn't, I'll have his teeth for piano keys. What time is it?'

In the faint glow from the dashboard, the driver consulted his watch. 'Eleven-forty, sir.'

'Bloody hell. I thought it was three in the morning.'

Pike said hopelessly, 'What are we meant to be looking out for?'

Nobody answered.

The tips of his fingers were starting to go dead. In another few moments the numbness would travel up both arms: to pre-empt the event, Pike sat upright and flexed each limb from the elbow, contriving in the process to deal the chief inspector alongside him a damaging blow to the ribs. Forester grunted.

'When you're quite finished.'

'I'm getting cramp.'

'Look on it as good practice for three in a cell.' The chief inspector sounded edgy. On the brink of a retort Pike changed his mind, subsided into his corner, contemplated with a wretched foreboding the message of the put-down he had just received. Loss of liberty. Confinement. Until now, the idea that such a fate might await him had merely skirted his subconscious: with its rise to the surface, like globs of sour cream on milk, came the certainty that under no imaginable circumstances would he be able to endure the ordeal. If it came about, he would go insane. His left hand stole towards the door catch. One wrench and he could be out of here, sprinting into the gloom, a fugitive but free. He might be caught—so what? There remained a fighting chance, and it was worth taking. *Now. Do it now.* His thigh-muscles clenched themselves. His wrist tautened. He gave the catch a sharp tug.

From the front, Inspector Morgan said peacefully, 'We've a special lock on that one, Mr Pike, you'll find. A safeguard for our rear-seat passengers—prevents them falling out. You can come a nasty cropper that way.' Abruptly his voice changed. 'Far end of the street. Anybody see what I do?'

Forester came alive with a jerk. He leaned across Pike's knees to peer into the blackness. 'Reckon it's what we're looking for?'

'It wobbled,' Morgan said cryptically. 'If it is, Steve Hewitt should be coming through any—'

As he spoke, the car's radio crackled. Morgan snatched at it. 'Alpha One to Delta Three. Is that what we think it is, just coming into Beech Close?'

A distorted male voice replied. 'Quite likely. We're approaching that area ourselves, keeping the subject in view. Standing well off, as instructed.'

'Grand. We don't want to rush things.' Morgan waited a moment. 'What's happening now?'

'Subject approaching the coach-house. Now level with it. Any visual contact your end?'

'Yes, we can see from here. Subject seems to have come to a standstill. Looks promising.'

Chief Inspector Forester breathed stertorously into Pike's ear. 'Lousy view from here,' he said fretfully. 'What's going on.'

Morgan said helpfully, 'Far as I can see, the lamp's being aimed down on to the road surface.' He glanced round between the seat-backs. 'Too soon, would you think?'

Forester scraped his jawline with two fingernails. 'No, to hell with it. Tell 'em to move in.'

'Action now,' Morgan snapped into the radio.

Wrenching life into the engine, the driver swung the Rover out from its hideaway and took it screamingly in bottom gear towards the mouth of the drive. Simultaneously, Pike saw, the headlamps of another car had shone out suddenly from the farther end of Beech Close and were closing in, the twin beams bouncing as the front wheels hit the ruts. Between the two vehicles, the lesser beam from the lamp quivered and swung like a theatre spotlight stalking some elusive performer from wing to wing, before twisting violently to aim itself at a nearby laurel hedge as the figure manipulating it made an attempt to cut and run. Escape was foiled easily. Already the second car, lurching to a halt in a grinding of pebbles, had disgorged a pair of animated police uniforms which needed only to station themselves in the path of flight to bring off a smooth interception. Forester, still vibrating Pike's starboard eardrum, uttered his satisfaction.

'Now,' he declared, with more emphasis than originality. 'We'll see what we shall see.'

Thrusting open his door, he stepped out stiffly to join the two constables who between them were holding an unresisting bundle, now clearly illuminated by the glare from the two vehicles. From where he sat, Pike had an unblocked view of thick-knit sweater, trousers, and a cap or beret; identification, however, remained a struggle. The voice was the giveaway.

'What's the idea, then? What's going on?'

Chief Inspector Forester seized his cue adroitly. 'Funny you should ask that, Miss Franklin. I was about to put the selfsame question to you.'

The bicycle was wheeled on to the footway and propped against a tree. Meanwhile, more headlamps and the distant, deep-throated bellow of an engine proclaimed the approach of further mechanized interference with the urban nocturnal serenity. Pike sat numbly watching events. He had listened to Inspector Morgan talking again into the radio, instructing Steve to inform Mr Plymstock that he could move his chap in now, thanks very kindly, as soon as he liked. Now, through the Rover's open rear door, the unhurried voice of Forester came through to them from the kerbside.

'I'm still waiting, Miss Franklin, for a convincing explanation. Just what were you up to—a girl of nineteen on a pedal cycle—prowling around this part of the world at midnight?'

'Any law against it?'

'There's no specific law against a lot of things. But I'm still entitled to look into them. Searching for something, were you? Something you might have dropped?'

'None of your business.'

'Since we're talking about laws, let me remind you there's nothing illegal about losing things and then going back to find 'em.' As the decibels from the advancing motor multiplied, the chief inspector progressively raised his voice to compete. 'So why not tell us about it? We might be able to help.'

'Get knotted.' The girl's voice was shaky but defiant. 'I was just out for a ride. I stopped 'cos I was out of breath. Anything wrong with that?'

Forester turned to gaze along the street. 'Level going,' he observed mildly. 'Why the sudden big lung-collapse, here of all places?'

'I've just come six miles, that's why.'

'Seems a lot of exertion to indulge in, this time of night.'

'I couldn't sleep.'

'Oh? Something on your mind?'

A scattering of residents in diverse modes of nightwear had appeared at garden gateways to rivet their gazes to the spectacle. Unbidden, the two constables had moved in opposite directions to contain them. The arrival of the appliance to which the earsplitting diesel motor belonged was the signal for a flutter of excitement to travel from group to group. The engine-note dipped to a fierce throb. Forester, for the moment, ignored its presence.

'You see, Miss Franklin, I'm doing my best to understand. I know you use the bike to work, but you wouldn't classify yourself as a racing cyclist, I fancy? Or a keep-fit fanatic? What made you, on this particular night, head this way and start investigating the road surface?'

Gail offered no reply. With a puckered nose, she was staring at the giant excavator now stationary at the spot, panting like a parched antelope at a watering hole, the legend A. J. PLYMSTOCK CONTRACTORS painted along its flank. Up in the cab, the silhouette of its operator's head and shoulders could be discerned. Pivoting at last, Forester sent him a wave. The operator killed the motor, swarmed out, climbed down to road level.

'What's the form, then, Guvnor?'

'Sorry about the overtime,' Forester returned genially, 'but your boss assured me you wouldn't mind, actually.'

'My pleasure. Where'd you want us to start?'

The chief inspector considered the loose stone and gravel of the roadway, eyed the bicycle, turned back to glance at the girl. Making his decision, he pointed.

'There,' he suggested.

After an hour's deafening work, the spoil deposited behind the swivelling torso of the excavator had grown to a hillock, while the cavity in front of it deepened and expanded by the minute.

To Pike, watching dazedly, it began to seem that he had been sitting there for weeks, following passively the course of some sequence of events that he had helped to fashion before unaccountably losing control of, weakly handing it over to others to bring to a conclusion as macabre as it was somehow predictable. Gail, he noticed when he remembered to look, remained hunched silently on the low stone wall protecting the front garden of the coach-house, closely flanked by Inspector Morgan with an air of protectiveness that was engaging if illusory. The din of the extraction process dominated everything. Load followed load from hole to heap. Signs of restiveness began to emanate from the chief inspector. Stepping forward at last, he gestured to the operator.

'How far down?'

'Just getting under the pipe, guvnor.'

'Take it easy. We don't want—'

'Hang about.'

Stabilizing the machine, the man cut the motor, swung himself out of the cab once more, clambered down to approach the lip of the crater. He peered over.

Forester went forward to join him. 'Spotted something?'

The operator pointed.

Standing beside him, looking down, the chief inspector commenced a slow nodding of the head that suggested a degree of self-satisfaction leavened by regret.

'Right,' he said quietly. 'You can back up now, thanks. We'll take over from here.'

## CHAPTER 16

The full statement made ultimately by Gail Franklin caused a major and lasting sensation locally, as well as an ephemeral one nationally, when the case came to court.

'Gareth and me had been going together for a fair bit, up until the time he gave us the brush-off.

'He was seeing Arlene Pike, too. I knew that, because I kept watch once or twice when she went to his house of a night. I used to bike over there to see what was going on, like. They never knew I was around. I'd slip in the back way, round by the gate, and look through the glass door into the living-room. I didn't much fancy what I saw. It made me very depressed.

'Marvin—Arlene's husband—was getting a bit down, too, about this time. He reckoned Gareth was swindling him over the business, which I wouldn't be surprised if he was. Apart from that, he'd started getting suspicious of the pair of them—Arlene and Gareth. I felt sorry for him. I knew how he felt.

'I reckoned I might be able to help, and do myself a favour at the same time. I thought, if Arlene went back to Marvin, me and Gareth could sort of get together again, take up where we'd left off. I still loved him and I wanted to marry him. I thought p'raps he'd just got this thing about Arlene. I thought, if she went back to her husband, Gareth might sort of forget her in a little while and come back to me.

'Then one day, Marvin spoke to me about Gareth. He said he reckoned he'd got proof that Gareth was rooking him over the stock, and I could see he was wondering about the best way of using it so as to stop his game and at the same time p'raps do somethink about Arlene. From the way he spoke, I could tell he was still fond of her, like.

'I spent the rest of the day thinking about it. By the time we shut the shop, I'd got something worked out.

'That night I told my mum and dad I was going over to my friend Rosemary's place to do some recording and that. I'd done it before, so they never took much notice. Only this time, after I'd left the house, I biked over to Gareth's place to have it out with him.

'I guessed Arlene might be there, but I didn't let that put me off. I reckoned if I told them both what Marvin knew, they might panic a bit, and Arlene might decide to give Gareth up. I figured it was worth a try.

'As it turned out, though, Arlene wasn't there. Gareth was surprised to see me, but he invited me in and we had this quite friendly chat, to start with. I explained about Marvin and said I didn't think he'd do anythink about the stock swindle as long as he got Arlene back, and I wouldn't say anything myself if Gareth and me got together again.

'He didn't fancy the idea. I could see that. He sort of pretended to consider it, but he never fooled me. All the time, he was trying to think of another way out. It was obvious.

'Anyway, while we was talking, the phone rang and it was Marvin. Gareth spoke to him for a bit, then hung up and told me it looked as if Arlene had walked out and he couldn't say he blamed her. He said, *She'll be shacking up with me now, like we always planned. Get the message, sweetheart?* He used to talk like that, sort of tough-guy only he wasn't, if you get what I mean. He was a coward, really. I knew that.

'So then I got nastier, like. I'd not meant to, only he got my back up, made me feel all funny inside, like as if I'd eaten something that had turned on me.

'I told him he was a devil and a monster. That made him laugh. Not nicely . . . more in a sneering kind of a way. He said I was a spotty little adolescent fool and he didn't know why he'd ever put up with me for five minutes. On and on like this, till I lost control of myself.

'I had these scissors in my bag. I'd taken them from the display rack in the shop that afternoon, meaning to show him the price-tag and ask him why we was charging more for them than the Patels down the road—because I reckoned he'd picked up the difference somehow and I wanted to show him I wasn't kidding when I said we'd got proof. I can remember fetching them out of the bag, but after that it's all a bit hazy.

'I think Gareth tried to get away through the glass door. I must have gone after him and just sort of lashed out with my right hand. I wanted to wipe the smile off his face. I wanted to hurt him. He had his back to me, I remember that.

'There was this kind of fog and these sounds inside my head. Next time I looked, he was lying there on the paving slabs just outside the door. He was on his stomach with his legs stretched out, and there was blood on his shirt.

'I never felt queasy or anything. I felt quite calm. First of all I made sure there was no signs of me ever being in the room: there wasn't a lot needed doing, because I'd not eaten or drunk anything, or even sat down. I still had my jacket on. I always wear a jacket when I bike.

Makes it easier to keep your bag slung on your shoulder and it's never too hot—specially at night. I always like to take my bag. You never know what you might be needing.

'After I'd seen to the room, I was going to mess it up a bit, like, make it look as if there'd been a fight. I thought I could make it seem as if some burglar had got in from the garden and caught Gareth off his guard. This was a bit after midnight. I reckoned that should add up okay. It was just a matter of me getting away without being seen.

'I'd left the bike outside in the front garden, against a bush. Just as I came out, I heard the sound of this engine along the street, so I hid behind the bush and waited.

'Marvin's van went by and turned in at the drive, the one leading to Gareth's back garden. I recognized the van. You can't mistake it—there's a darker patch along the side where Marvin painted out the name of the bloke who had it before. He never got around to putting MARGAR instead.

'I thought he must have come to have it out with Gareth, too. It got me in a bit of a state. I wasn't sure what to do. I couldn't get back inside the house from the front, seeing as I'd shut the door. So I wheeled the bike round to the drive. I don't really know why, but I suppose I wanted to see what Marvin did.

'The van was pulled up right by the gate; I saw the inside light come on, so I knew Marvin had got out. Otherwise I couldn't see anything much. It struck me as funny that he hadn't gone straight to the front door and rung, or something. I heard him opening the back doors to the van, but I still couldn't see, so I left the bike behind another bush and crept nearer.

'Marvin was having a struggle and he never spotted me,

so I was able to get quite close. It was Arlene he was carrying. He had her across his shoulder, ever so limp, and I guessed she was a goner. He took her through the gate and I expected him to turn right, towards the house, only he didn't. He lugged her to the end of the garden and dumped her. Then he got a shovel from the shed and started digging this hole.

'By this time I'd guessed what he was up to. It took him a while to get the hole big enough, but finally he sort of rolled her into it and covered her up. When he'd finished, I thought he'd go straight back to the van, but instead he went towards the house.

'I reckoned he was sure to come across Gareth. There didn't seem to be anythink I could do. I just went on waiting.

'When he came back to the gate, though, he never looked any different. I mean, I couldn't see his expression, it was too dark, but he was walking exactly the same, not hurrying that much, though he wasn't hanging about, either. He just shut the gate, got back in the van and drove off. I was hiding behind a tree, so he never saw me.

'While he was burying Arlene, I'd crept up to the van and hidden the scissors under the carpet by the driver's seat. It was sort of done on impulse. By then I was really scared. Lost my head a bit. Why I hid the scissors there I don't know, except that I thought p'raps it might be a good way to throw suspicion off myself. It was a stupid thing to do, 'cos I didn't want Marvin to get blamed for killing Gareth. I wanted people to think it was a burglar.

'Only, what with him coming along with Arlene and burying her like that, I got confused. By the time my head cleared and I was thinking properly again, Marvin had driven off in the van and it was too late to get the scissors back.

'Anyhow, I reckoned I could pick them up later. The main thing was, I'd thought of an idea about Gareth.

'Marvin's plan was pretty obvious. He wanted the cops to find Arlene's body buried in the garden so they'd think Gareth had killed her. But by then, of course, Gareth was dead too. I knew that, only Marvin didn't. At least I didn't think he knew.

'So I thought to myself: Why not let the police think it was Arlene who killed Gareth?

'She could just as easily have gone to see him that night as I did. They could have quarrelled and she could have stabbed him with the scissors. She'd as much chance as me, nearly, of whipping them from the shop. Then she could have run off and disappeared. As long as she wasn't found, they couldn't ever prove she'd not done it.

'The problem was, if she stayed where she was they'd find her, easy. She needed to be somewhere else.

'This was when I remembered about the pipes. They was laying them all along Beech Chase, digging these great trenches and shoving the pipes in, then filling up again with stones and gravel and that. They'd been doing it round our way, too, just lately. I'd watched them at it. Sometimes they laid the pipes and filled in again all on the same day, but quite often I noticed they left the filling-in till the next morning. So the trench was left open overnight, with the pipe at the bottom.

'I thought they might have done this near Gareth's place, so I went back to have a look. And they had. Nearly opposite his front garden there was this deep hole with the new pipe leading into it and a big pile of stones dumped close by. I reckoned they'd be filling it in again pretty soon.

'It was chancy, all right, but it was all I could think of. There wasn't much time.

'I went back to the garden with the bike and got the shovel out of the shed. It didn't take long to dig Arlene out —Marvin hadn't buried her that deep. Luckily she didn't weigh much, either. And I'm used to shifting loads about. I've handled worse than her in the shop.

'After I'd levelled the ground a bit, I got her onto the bike, over the saddle, and managed to wheel her back up the drive to the street. All this time I never saw nobody. It's a deadbeat neighbourhood anyway, and that time of night there wasn't a soul around. So I got her to the hole okay, and tipped her in.

'She landed slap next to the pipe, sort of half underneath it, which I reckoned was a slice of luck. To be on the safe side, though, I went back for the shovel and used it to chuck some stones over the edge.

'It took quite a while, 'cos I had to work as quietly as I could. In the end I'd a fair-sized heap down there, so I climbed down myself and spread them all over her. By the time I'd finished there was no sign of her. To my way of thinking, it looked just as if the men had left it like that so as the rest of the stones could be poured in next morning.

'Well, the same morning, really. It was getting on for two-thirty when I climbed back out and I was dead tired, really knackered, but I reckoned I'd done a good job.

'There wasn't any more I could do except cross my fingers. I took the shovel back to the shed, then biked home. It was turned three when I got in, but my mum and dad never heard me. They're both heavy sleepers. I told them at breakfast I'd been with Rosemary till quite late, and they never showed much interest.

'Then came the hard part—carrying on that day like it was normal. Up until half way through the morning I never knew if they'd found Gareth or dug up Arlene, or anything. I just had to put a face on it.

'The worst moment was when the sergeant come round

to the shop. My heart nearly stopped beating. I was afraid they'd found Arlene . . . but it was Gareth he'd called about. Marvin and me had to answer all sorts of questions. I'd known about Arlene and Gareth, I told him, but I didn't think Marvin had. I said a lot of other things, too, with the idea of putting the finger on Arlene.

'The cops still had their suspicions, though. Of Marvin, not me. The chief inspector saw him that afternoon and really zonked into him, from what I heard.

'Earlier on, I'd tried to get into the van for the scissors, but no luck. Marvin had left it parked round the service road at the back, with the doors locked. When I asked for the keys, he wanted to know what I was fetching out of it. I couldn't think of nothing, so I made some excuse and decided to try and pinch the keys from his jacket when I got the chance. Only I never did. He kept it on the whole time, right up until he had to hand the keys over to the chief inspector, and that did it. They found the scissors straight away.

'So I just had to hope they might think it was Arlene who'd left them there. It meant she'd have to have gone back home after killing Gareth, planted the scissors and then gone off again . . . which didn't seem too likely but at least it was possible. It all depended, though, whether the police thought she'd properly vanished or not.

'I couldn't hardly wait for closing time. Luckily I didn't have to, because Marvin shut the shop early. So in the afternoon, while he was busy with the Chief at the station, I was able to bike over to Beech Chase for a recce.

'There was a cop car parked outside the house and a copper at the front door, but nobody took any notice of me. I just went by slowly on the bike and had a quick look. And it was okay. They'd filled the hole in and smoothed the road over, then gone off to start on another trench farther along —quite some distance.

'I felt so relieved, I nearly cried. I went straight back and got ready to help out Marvin as much as I could. I wanted to do my best for him, 'cos he'd always been decent to me.'

## CHAPTER 17

'All of which,' Chief Inspector Forester observed to Pike before the trial, 'was fine and dandy—as far as it went.'

'Meaning?'

'Meaning that as long as your busy young shop assistant remained confident that your wife Arlene was safely interred under a ton of rubble and a twenty-foot section of water main, we were going to have our job cut out to prove her involvement.'

'What made you suspect her, in the first place?' Pike put the question in the certainty that it would get a considered reply. A curious rapport had built up between himself and the chief inspector, traceable from the moment when the latter had announced his intention in Pike's case to go for manslaughter only, on the grounds of extreme provocation, albeit a further charge of unlawful disposal of the body was unavoidable. Not all detectives of medium-high rank, Pike had decided, were necessarily ogres. Nor did a ginger complexion invariably denote hot-headed obduracy. You had to take people as you found them.

'What put us on to her?' Forester sniffed. 'A guy like your partner, Pikey, doesn't race a string of fillies in total secrecy, you know. Even in nice, secluded backwaters like Beech Chase, people tend to sit up and take notice. At the time Somers was seeing your Miss Franklin, one or two of the neighbours were discreetly marking her arrival at his house

on her bike. In due course, they were only too ready and
willing to describe her.'

'They would be.'

Another sniff came from Forester. 'The same goes for
your wife. Also they were able to provide details of the van.
An observant bunch, our suburban population. When it
suits them to be.'

'They don't seem to have noticed much when it really
mattered.'

'As luck would have it,' the chief inspector explained,
'our prime informant was away on holiday at the time.
Coupled with the fact that it was all happening in the small
hours of a moonless night, it does go a long way to account
for both yourself and Miss Franklin having such a clear
run.'

Pike grunted. 'Okay. So it didn't take you long to find
out that Gail had been on Gareth's . . . guest-list. What put
you wise to the rest of it?'

'You did.'

'Me?'

'If you remember,' Forester said with a certain smugness,
'it was you who introduced Miss Franklin as an alibi for the
couple of hours after midnight when you claimed to be
driving around, looking for your wife . . .'

'I'm not likely to forget.'

'Well, naturally we ran a check. And quite frankly, very
little added up. Your wife's parents, for example: they
confirmed that you called on them, but your father-in-
law also told us that while he was phoning from upstairs
he had a clear view from the window of your van parked
outside—and he was perfectly sure Miss Franklin wasn't
in it.'

'She could have—'

'We also checked with Rosemary Shaw of River View,
the friend who Miss Franklin was supposed to have been

spending the evening with. She held out loyally for a while, but after various things had been pointed out to her she finally got the message and admitted that your assistant had never been there that night.'

'All right, but—'

'Whereupon, we questioned Miss Franklin's parents. They informed us their daughter went off on her bike that evening about ten o'clock, with a vague reference to visiting Miss Shaw . . . only she cycled off in the wrong direction. Her dad noticed it as he followed her out of the house to walk the dog. The route she actually took would have taken her towards Beech Chase, assuming she kept to it.'

'Nothing in any of that,' Pike scoffed.

'Taken individually,' said Forester, unruffled, 'nothing conclusive, I agree. Collectively, it was suggestive. Enough to make me take the precaution of putting a tail on the pair of you.'

'Charming.'

'You have to remember, I still didn't know at the time whether you were in cahoots. And at first it seemed you were, because practically the first place you headed for together was Beech Chase and your partner's back garden. My bloke radioed in, and as you know I managed to be there in time to study your reaction when you found your wife's body was gone.'

'What did you make of it?'

'Your reaction? Total incredulity.'

'What else did you expect?'

'I was doing my best,' Forester returned on a note of reproof, 'not to anticipate. Keeping an open mind, as ever. And you want to know what really intrigued me?'

'What?'

'The reaction of Miss Franklin. Now there was a case, if

ever I saw one, of somebody *trying* to look thunderstruck and not making much of a fist of it.'

'She could have been—'

'Too bemused by events to show a lot? Maybe. All the same, it set me thinking. Putting two and two together, as it were, and coming up with nine. On the strength of this, I reached a conclusion. I decided to try forcing the issue a little.'

'How?'

The chief inspector placed a finger to the side of his nose. 'It occurred to me,' he said complacently, 'that it might be no bad thing if an element of doubt were introduced into your assistant's very active mind. You see, I'd already made a note of those holes being dug in the road outside the coach-house. A fairly obvious possibility, wouldn't you agree?'

'If it was that obvious,' Pike said tartly, 'why didn't you get the digger along sooner and have it up?'

'Because we still wouldn't have been in a position to say for certain who'd buried your wife's body there. Re-buried it, rather. From your expression in the garden, I was pretty sure it wasn't you. Unless you'd done it in your sleep, which seemed improbable.'

'For a while, I did wonder—'

'That left Miss Franklin. If it was her, she'd know the precise spot where she dumped her, and she could save us a lot of unnecessary excavation while at the same time incriminating herself. So, I flew a small kite.'

'How small?'

'Detective-Inspector Morgan,' remarked Forester with apparent irrelevance, 'does rather a nice line in assumed voices. Hobby of his.'

'What's that to do with it?'

'Only that he seemed an apt candidate for the job. At my behest, he put a call through to Miss Franklin's home at

around eight-thirty that evening. Happily she was there and
he was able to speak to her. I dare say you can make a guess
at what he said?'

Pike shook his head.

'You'll never make a sleuth, Pikey. What he said was
something rather cryptic. Using his Irish navvy's voice—
one of his specialities—he told Miss Franklin: *Just a friendly
warning, my love. There's been a bit of a cave-in where they're laying
the pipes. They might have to scoop out and fill in again. Thought
you'd like to know.* Then he hung up.'

'I suppose you thought that was bloody clever?'

'I was quite pleased with it, actually. The more so, since
it had the desired effect. As you witnessed.'

'She might not have come running.'

'No. But she did, didn't she? She had to.'

'I'd have thought she'd have stayed away.'

'Not knowing what had happened? Fear, Pikey. That's
what dragged her back. She had to find out for herself
what had become of her precious tomb. Apart from
which . . .'

Pike cocked his chin. 'She might also,' the chief inspector
added, 'have been half-hoping to see whoever it was that
had rung her up.'

'Why would she want to do that?'

'So that she knew who she had to deal with. For all she
knew, it was a potential blackmailer—some workman on
the project, maybe. Or a night watchman who'd been on
site at the time in question and watched her dispose of
the corpse. And then perhaps followed her home by car.
Anything. She had to know the worst.'

'Okay, Chief. You were pretty smart.' Having thought it
over, Pike glanced up again. 'But why take me along to
watch the performance?'

Forester smiled. 'Just a final vetting of your reflexes. If
you had been responsible for transferring the body, after all,

obviously you'd have known the spot—and the chances are you'd have shown it. Plus, it was convenient to have you on hand to formally identify your wife when she was brought up.'

'You still weren't certain, then?'

'Certain?'

'Whether it was me or Gail, I mean. You couldn't bet on it, even then.'

'If I were to gamble,' Forester murmured, 'on any or all of the cases I deal with, I'd be bankrupt by now. I hope I've learned better. Certainly there was mighty little temptation to speculate on this one. Two corpses, two culprits. It's not often you stumble across a case of two violent deaths separately involving four interrelated people on the same night . . . practically a dead heat, you might say, and yet both more or less unpremeditated. Remarkable coincidence. At the same time,' added the chief inspector presently, 'you can see how it came about.'

Pike looked at him. 'Can you, Chief?'

'You might give me credit for a little perception, Pikey. I do know how pressure can build up.'

'You may know that, but there's still a fair bit you don't know.'

Forester's lean mouth twitched in some amusement. 'Such as what?'

'The real truth, for a start.'

'What are you on about now?'

'I've just told you. The truth. What was it you were saying, a moment ago? A remarkable coincidence. So it would have been, if that's the way it had happened. Only it wasn't.'

'Pike . . .'

'Sorry, Chief. I've been misleading you. It wasn't Gail who did it. She never stabbed my partner and then buried my wife in the street. It was me.'

'Now listen here . . .'

Pike quelled him with a flap of the hand. '*You* listen. I *was* at the coach-house that night, and I *did* stab Somers—before midnight. You were right about that, at least. I did make those phone calls from there. And I stowed the scissors in the van myself, meaning to get shot of them later, only in all the hurly-burly it went clean out of my head.' Shoulders hunched, Pike sat back wearily. 'I'm responsible for everything. Nobody else.'

For a few moments Chief Inspector Forester uttered no word. He sat in a frozen posture, dividing his attention between the backs of his own hands, appearing to find each of them of supreme fascination. Finally he moved. Planting an elbow on the desk, he used it for support in the course of a further intense survey, this time aimed at the midway point of Pike's jacket zip.

'Gail didn't do it, you say. Neither the killing of Somers, nor the redisposal of your wife's body afterwards?'

'Of course not. Had to be me, didn't it?'

'If you say so. One thing bothers me, though.'

Pike glanced up. 'And that is . . . ?'

'If it was you, then how come Gail knew just what part of the roadway to come along later and examine?'

Their eyes met. After a pause, Pike said, 'Simple. I'd told her.'

'You *told* her.' The chief inspector repeated the phrase lingeringly, as though testing it for texture and flavour. 'What for?'

'I had to confide in somebody.' Pike took a breath. 'Things were sort of closing in on me by that time . . . I needed advice. I reckoned Gail would stand by me, but not to the extent she did. I hadn't counted on that. Now I just want to set the record straight. Otherwise, the wrong person is going to stew in jail for something I did. I couldn't have that on my conscience.'

Forester grunted. 'Assuming that what you say is right, she's still an accessory after the fact.'

'The courts wouldn't be hard on her though, would they, Chief? I mean, she's just a kid. She couldn't be expected to have coped with a situation like that. She wouldn't have known what to do for the best.'

'She's got brains. She could have come to us.'

'But she wanted to protect me.'

'What, take some of the rap herself—knowing that you'd still be accused of strangling your wife?'

'She wasn't thinking straight, and besides—'

The rest of the sentence hiccoughed in Pike's throat as Chief Inspector Forester leapt to his feet. 'You're the one,' he exploded, 'who's not thinking straight. Why, Pike? What's made you spin me this rigmarole?'

'I've already explained. I don't want Gail locked up for—'

'Something she didn't do? No fear of that. She did it, all right.' Forester paced up and down, eyeing Pike with a mixture of scorn and exasperation. 'She's the one who stabbed Somers in a fit of jealousy, then did her best to chuck the blame on to your wife. Everything she's told us in that statement of hers stands up—make no mistake about that. We've checked it all, down to the last detail. So, Pike, I repeat: why are you wasting my time? Why this pathetic attempt at an eleventh-hour salvage operation on her behalf?'

Pike looked away and said nothing.

Resuming his chair, Forester sat regarding him in a kindlier manner. After a while he said, 'Quite fond of the young lady, aren't you?'

Pike gave a slight shake of the head. It was not a denial.

'Would I be right in thinking,' pursued the chief inspector, 'that there might be a couple of reasons for what you've just tried to do? One: you wanted to score with her, even more heavily than you seem to have done already. You're going to be jailed anyhow, so why not put up with a longer sentence in exchange for Gail's undying gratitude and affection? In the confident hope that she'll be there, waiting for you, when you finally get out. Something like that?'

Still Pike remained silent.

Releasing his own thumb, Forester tweaked his forefinger. 'Two: on a somewhat more practical note, could it be that you were hoping she might be able to keep the firm of Margar ticking over while you were inside, so you'd have something to go back to when you'd done your time? Or am I getting too fanciful?'

Pike stirred. 'No harm,' he mumbled, 'in looking to the future.'

'No harm at all. As long as you don't expect miracles.' Forester's survey became compassionate. 'Think about it, Pikey. Resourceful she may be, this teenage ex-assistant of yours, but does it seem likely, for a start, that she could run a newsagent's single-handed for several years—especially one that's already on the rocks? She'd need help, male help probably, and by the time you came back . . .' The chief inspector's gesture was eloquent. 'Feelings can change. At any age, and hers in particular. What it amounts to is, you'd have been putting your faith in moonshine.'

'Maybe. I reckoned it was worth a try.'

'Forget it. That's my advice. Wash your hands of her, just as she's now likely to wipe hers clean of you. I've seen this type of thing before, and believe me, it hardly ever works out.'

Pike glanced up. 'There's always the exception.'

Forester started to say something, caught himself, began again. 'You're determined to keep hoping she'll still be carrying a torch for you by the time you're both free to get together again? A girl who's shown she can be ruthless when provoked? A man-killer?'

Heaving himself upright in his chair, Pike shrugged. 'Right now, Chief, it's all I have to cling to. What have I got to lose?'